LCB

Married to A BALLA

A NOVEL BY

Jackie D.

Married
to
A BALLA

A Novel By:
Jackie D.

Life Changing Books in conjunction with Power Play Media
Published by Life Changing Books
P.O. Box 423 Brandywine, MD 20613

Library of Congress Cataloging-in-Publication Data;

www.lifechangingbooks.net
13 Digit: 978-1934230299
10 Digit: 1-934230294

Dedication

This book is dedicated to my son **Emanuel "Poobie" Chapman**. Words can't express how much I love you. I'm so proud of you and all your accomplishments. Never stop striving for your goals. Thanks for being my backbone. You gave me the will to push forward even at the times when I thought I couldn't make it.

Acknowledments

To my family, my sister Michelle Davis, my brother Charlie Davis, my half brother in NJ, Todd Sherman, my niece Jasmine Harris@ Elizabeth City State University. My nephews, Carlo Merritt and Montana Davis, my wonderful father Charles "Snoop" Davis and my step mom Michelle Peebles and my step sister Mikiya Peebles. Thanks for all the support; I love you ALL so much.

To my mother **Janelle "DC Reds" Davis** and my grandmothers **Ruth Martin** and **Marguerite Davis**, RIP, I miss you dearly.

To **Joel Miles**, aka Bobby James, and **Dezmine Wells**, I wish you both much success on your careers. I love you and thank you for having Poob's back. Real friends are hard to come by and you two have definitely ALWAYS been in his corner.

Also I would like to say thank you **to North Carolina Central University** in Durham, NC along with Coach **Levelle Moton** and the entire coaching staff for giving my son an opportunity, "trust me... you have a **"STAR"** and won't be disappointed!!

To my cousins, David "Mookie" Washington, Marcus Washington, JR. Davis and sons, Marcus Davis and family, Jennifer Wilder Davis and family, Tenika and Patrice Jefferson and family, Fred Lott and family, Dwight and Dana Peebles and family, Arnetta Jones and family and Shalonda Johnson and Family.

To my Uncles and Aunts, Dennis Davis, Carol Davis,

Louis Davis, Wayne Wilson, Loretta Martin, Arthur Washington, Marguerite Peebles, Dwight Peebles, Jennie Jefferson, Hubert Jefferson, Brenda Rand Davis. RIP Jackie Washington, Marlene Short.

To all my friends that have shown me so much love and support....Thanks and I love you!

Author Tonya Ridley, where do I begin? First off I would like to thank you for all that you have done for Poob and I over our thirty year friendship. And second I would like to thank you for introducing me to Azarel and Life Changing books. Never in my wildest dreams did I think we would go from avid book readers who discussed and got mad at the characters in other peoples books (like the shit was for real) to actually writing our own novels. Thanks for all your help with *Love Heist* and *Married to a Balla*. Josh is lucky to have a sister like you in his life. I love you and wish you much success.

Author Danette Majette, who would've thought, that me picking you up from the airport when you had nobody else to call, would produce such a wonderful friendship. You're such a beautiful person inside and out and I thank you for being there for me and listening to my cries this past year when I was about to lose my MIND! I love you. Thanks for all your help with this book. Whew, it got a little rough at times but you helped me stay focused! We hit almost every set in NC promoting our books and I look forward to doing it again with our new books. Shouts out to our new business, The Literary Connection! www.literaryconnection.net

Marketa "Kee Kee" Salley, it's time to get back on that court girly. Bryan Majette, your mother loves and misses her son! Shout out to Cousin Shelley Majette Carrington.

Sharon Kirkley, we've been friends for so many years I've lost count. I love you and I'm so glad to have you as my friend. Keep searching, its coming boo boo!

Author Tiphani Montgomery, thanks for listening when I needed to vent and never ever changing up on me. Also thanks for all your help with *Love Heist*...Rule the World Baby!! LOL

Carla Williams-Johnson, (Durham, NC) and **Chanda Zigler Davis**, even though we don't talk every day, our friendship has always been genuine, and I love y'all for life.

Joe Guzman and Isaiah "Eben" Fuller, thanks for the support!!

Chris Currie, let's go...TS baby!!, Joy Avery, Nikki, Willis, Yvette Jones, Barbara Benjamin, Carla Johnson, Michelle "Mi Mi" Parham, D 'Juan Laws, Kym Johnson, Pam "Pee Wee" Wells, Jazmine Wilson, Annette James, Frances Pulley, Tanya Pulley, Ciarra Wall, John Wall, Kadedra Jacobs, Ryce Hatchett, Allison " Moo Moo" Elliott, Nia Hill, Nicole "Nikki Rochelle, Gillie and Keisha, Brooks, To Laniesha and The Entire Merritt family, Lativia " Libby" Pinkney, Allison Mitchell, Ayana Knight, Sherry Richburg, Karen Hodges, Big Mike, Ramona Myers, Tracey Jones, Chyna Mike, Krista Stallings- Hodges, Talk of the Town Hair Salon, Bell, Brandy, Trina, Steve and Chajuan. Kuniki Tabb-Parks and family, Melvin Tabb, I love you boy! Tyler Griffis, CJ Wilkinson, Big Play Ray Willis and the rest of the NCCU basketball team.

Big Tex and Shy @ The Star Bar, To Rob "Man" Williams and family, Nadine Allen, Tiny Williams, Sophia Williams and Jason and Nakkia Barnett, to the membership crew at my job NCMS, Shawn, Kristen, Lauren, Richard, and Garry and Jennifer Soboleski thanks for always having my back when I would drag into work tired as hell from staying up all night working on chapters. Deanna Godwin, Yahaira "Ya Ya" Botello, Kelly Wilson and Candice Wright, to the crew at the Wake Co. Prenatal Clinic, to Gwen Crawford and Danya Perry@ CIS, to Author Lamont LP Pettiway and Author Chakara in Raleigh, NC keep doing your thing. To the Entire Tucker family, I got you Pop Tucker, To Big Poobie Chapman, and the entire Chapman family in NJ, Stephon "Fat" Lawrence, Rodney " Box" McClamb and family, Mike "Dot"

Phillips and family, to the Satterfield family, Sylvia Vaughn and all my friends/coworkers @ The Vesta and Buck Jones group homes.

To all my friends and former classmates at Enloe High School, you have really shown me love and I really appreciate it.

To my friends on lock down, Face, Black, Beefy, Salom, Rhamel, Little E, and all the other inmates that are reading my books, thank you!

To any of my family or friends that I might have missed, I love you and please forgive me.

A special shout out to all the distributors and independent book stores that helped promote my book in any way. Quita @TLJ, Mondell Pope and all the Urban Knowledge locations, DC Book Diva, all The Books a Million stores, Black and Nobel in Philly, Novel Tees, and the rest of the book stores that showed me love. Thank you!

To Azarel, the best boss lady in the world, thanks again for allowing me to publish another book and to be part of the Life Changing Books family. You're such an inspiration to me.

Leslie Allen, aka the night owl. Words can't even express how much I appreciate you. Thanks for all your help with *Love Heist* and now *Married to a Balla*. You're the bomb, girl!!

To the test readers, Ashaundria and Virginia, thank you. To Keisha George, and Tamara Lee @ Hush Boutique, some of the hottest clothes around! Also, thanks to Kellie for the hot cover.

To my fellow authors of LCB ..... Tonya Ridley, Danette Majette, VegasClarke, CJ Hudson, Tiphani Montgomery, J. Tremble, Miss KP, Carla Pennington, Ericka Williams, Kendall Banks, Capone, Mike Warren, Chantel Jolie, Sasha Raye, C. Stecko, and anyone else on the team that I missed...it has truly been a blessing to work with such a great group of people! LCB for Life, let's get this money!

Lastly…. to all the people that purchased my first novel, thank you….I received nothing but positive feedback from all of you and I hope you will continue to follow me. Be on the lookout for my next one.

Check me out at:
http://www.facebook.com/loveheist
twitter.com/basketballmom09
www.theliteraryconnection.net

Peace and Blessing
Jackie D.

Chapter One

Skye smiled as she maneuvered through the large crowd of guests attending her husband's all white affair. Just like all the other parties she threw, Skye made sure the celebration in their breathtaking six bedroom Palm Island estate was first class by hiring one of Miami's top event planners. From the ritzy décor, and elaborate food to the aggressive security guards enforcing the all white dress code, the gathering would definitely be considered 'party of the year.' With Sandino celebrating his thirty-fifth birthday, Skye spared no expenses. Other than the nosey neighbors calling the police due to all the traffic, it was an affair renowned in elegance and glamour. Skye just prayed her husband was impressed and the get-together would help rebuild their relationship.

She watched as some of the guests lounged on the oversized white couches in the backyard as the other 200 VIP guests which included professional ball players, rappers and A-list actors were treated to a live band. It was a warm September night, perfect for anyone enjoying the ocean breeze or looking up at the blanket of stars.

Everything seemed to be perfect until Skye spotted Sandino, his boy Black and two Spanish-looking females in short skimpy dresses chatting by the bar.

Her mood changed instantly.

After grabbing a glass of champagne off one of the

waiter's trays, Skye quickly downed it before directing her attention back to the obvious groupies. By this time, the taller woman was dancing up against her husband's leg. Even though she was pissed, Skye had to admit, Sandino did look extra good for the event, so she could understand the woman's attraction.

With a chestnut brown complexion, jet black curly hair and a neatly trimmed beard, Sandino was the true definition of tall dark and handsome. Standing at 6'4 and 295 lbs, his stocky football player build along with a perfect porcelain veneer smile always seemed to turn women on. His sense of style didn't hurt either. The twelve carat black ice diamond chain he wore gleamed against his white Fedora linen suit that Skye had custom made. It was hard keeping women off of her man, which had worn on Skye after fourteen years of marriage.

Trying not to ruin the party, Skye decided to keep her cool instead of approaching Sandino. However, she didn't know how long her calm demeanor would last as she watched the foursome leave the bar then walk into one of the custom white tents.

"So, you're just gonna stand there while your husband flirts with other bitches?"

When Skye turned around, her friend Asia stood there with a disappointed glare. "Please don't start."

Asia threw both her hands in the air. "Skye, don't act like you don't see what the hell is going on. Why are you standing here acting like you're the sideline chick? You're his damn wife."

"I'm aware of that, Asia."

"Then go find out what the hell is going on. One of them could have their ass up in the air by now."

Skye shook her head. It was hard trying to be a lady or turn the other cheek when Sandino was constantly being disrespectful, but on the other hand she also knew there would be consequences if she caused a scene in front of his friends.

Her attention was suddenly shifted when she looked up and noticed their nanny Ms. Petra in the window holding four-month old Payton, the newest addition to the Washington family. Ms. Petra was an older, heavy-set woman from Jamaica with long thick dreads that had grown drastically over the years. Not only had Ms. Petra helped Skye raise her two boys, but she was also one hell of a housekeeper. Over the years Ms. Petra and Skye developed a bond and she often consoled her through the difficult times with Sandino.

With Skye losing her parents in a car accident at an early age, she considered Ms. Petra a mother figure. Over time though, Sandino grew jealous of their relationship and threatened to fire Ms. Petra on several occasions. Luckily his threats were never carried out because along with Skye, her sons Kareem and Jordan, considered her as part of the family. Plus her cooking was out of this world. There was no way anyone could part with her famous jerk chicken and dumplings.

Suddenly, Kareem and Jordan appeared in the window, too. After waving at them, Skye smiled at her sons. She loved them and tried her best to shield the two teenagers from some of the horrible things going on in their home. Living with their father hadn't always proven to be the best life due to Sandino's strict ways. He'd made it clear on several occasions that they were to follow in his footsteps by playing sports. It could be either football or basketball since he was a fan of both, but they had to be athletic. His famous line was, "ain't no punk-ass sissys being raised up in this house!"

Sandino even insisted on naming the kids after his favorite basketball players, Michael Jordan, Kareem Abdul Jabbar, and also the late great football star, Walter Payton. Skye had no choice in the matter and was forced to give into his demands as always.

As Ms. Petra and the kids disappeared, Skye began to think about her life, and how she prayed almost every night that things would go back to her and Sandino's days at Morgan

State University. He'd gone from this sweet, gentle guy who walked her to class everyday to someone she barely knew. Even when Skye found out she was pregnant during her sophomore year, Sandino never left her side. He was always a kind and supportive man who treated Skye with the up-most respect. Someone she fell deeply in love with. Their love for each other still seemed to flourish after their second son was born two years later and Sandino was drafted by the NFL. They even got married during his first year in the league.

However, their marital bliss seemed to hit a brick wall once Sandino received a severe knee injury four years ago. Once he was placed on the injured reserve list, the stress of not being able to play football began tearing their family apart, especially when Sandino started abusing the pain killer, Oxycontin.

His addiction soon produced violent mood swings and in time had them all walking around on egg shells not knowing when he would have an outburst. Although intense physical therapy eventually led Sandino back on the field, he'd been traded to three different teams due to his attitude. He'd only played with the Dolphins one year, and they'd already threatened to trade him once again if he didn't get himself together. Apparently all the fines for late practices and arguing with the defensive coordinator wasn't working. To make matters worse, he'd already been suspended for an illegal hit during the first preseason game. Only Skye and a few others knew he was a functioning drug addict who knew how to pass drug tests. Skye often wondered if she would ever see the man she once knew and loved surface before it was too late.

"Excuse me, Mrs. Washington, I'm so sorry," a waiter said bumping into her.

Skye came out the daze making sure he hadn't spilled champagne on her white silk Missoni dress which fit her body like a glove. At a toned weight of a hundred and thirty-five pounds, it was hard to believe she'd birthed three kids.

"What up ladies?" Skye heard someone say.

When she turned around, Sandino's friend, Cruze was turning up a glass of Hennessey and Coke. They'd been good friends since knee-high.

"Hey Cruze," Asia spoke in a ghetto tone. She'd been trying to get with him forever, but he never seemed interested.

Cruze only nodded at Asia before directing his attention back to Skye. "You out did yourself on the party. This shit is banging."

"Thanks, your boy just headed over there," Skye said, pointing in the direction of the tents.

"Alright, I'ma holla at you a little later." Cruze gave her a small peck on the cheek before walking away.

Cruze, who'd just started growing dreads, was an average looking guy, but his rock hard one hundred and eighty pound body and swag were out of this world. It caused the women to flock to him like crazy.

Out of all Sandino's friends, Skye liked Cruze the most. Although he'd gotten into some trouble and spent a short time in prison, he'd always seemed to be a positive figure in Sandino's life. Never one of his "yes" men, Cruze was the only person willing to stand up to Sandino and tell him when he was wrong. He also had admiration for their marriage, and didn't condone Sandino's bad-boy ways. Skye could only hope some of Cruze's good ways rubbed off on her husband.

"Damn, that nigga must stay in the gym," Asia said. "Maybe I'll ask if he needs some company one day."

"Let's go inside," Skye quickly suggested. She didn't even wait for Asia's response before she headed inside their 6,800 square foot home.

After socializing all evening, Skye desperately needed to sit down and rest her feet. *Damn these Giuseppe sandals are killing me. For $700 dollars they should have a damn foot massager built inside,* Skye thought.

As soon as she plopped down at the huge maple leaf

granite bar in the kitchen, Asia walked in behind her wearing a tight fitting black Theory jumpsuit showing off her flat stomach and bodacious set of hips. Asia was your classic pretty girl with flawless brown skin, hazel eyes and was always dressed to kill…just like Skye. In fact the two had even met inside the Coral Gables Neiman Marcus store a few years ago. Asia who had just moved to Miami from Texas asked Skye her advice about a Louis Vuitton purse that she was about to buy. Normally, Skye didn't hold conversations with unknown women, especially stuck-up Neiman Marcus ones, but it was something about Asia that instantly made Skye put her guards down.

After exchanging numbers, the two hit it off instantly and went on massive shopping sprees during Sandino's away games, and Skye even managed to sneak out a few times to go with Asia to the hottest clubs. What Skye didn't know at first was that Asia was a party girl who loved to be on every set. Even though Skye felt like Asia acted like all the rest of Miami's groupie chicks at times, she was still good people.

"Skye, you really know how to throw a party, although Sandino's ungrateful-ass doesn't deserve it, or you for that matter," Asia stated.

"Asia, please, I asked you not to start tonight. My fucking feet hurt and I'm not in the mood. Plus you know I had to beg him to let you come tonight," Skye responded. Sandino hated Asia's whorish ways as well.

Asia rolled her eyes. She hated the way Skye let him control her. She didn't care how much money he had. In her heart, Skye could do much better. "Fuck Sandino. He may own you, but he don't own me. When do you plan to leave? I see that mark under your eye that you're trying to hide."

Skye bit her bottom lip. She thought the concealer she'd put on had covered her newest war wound.

"Is this where the real party is?" a male voice suddenly interrupted.

Skye and Asia both smiled at the handsome, light-skinned brotha standing in the kitchen doorway wearing what looked like a white Versace suit.

"Party over hurrr!" Asia yelled raising her hands in the air with her drink. "Damn, he's a looker," she whispered. "Who is he?" Every now and then her country Texas slang would come out.

"That's Keon, Sandino's new trainer. He trains all the top ball players in the league. He's defiantly paid. I saw him pull up in the new Porsche Panamera."

"Damn, hook me up Skye," Asia replied.

When Keon walked in the kitchen and joined the ladies, Asia licked her full lips. *Yeah, I knew that was Versace,* she thought getting a closer look at his suit.

"Keon, this is my good friend Asia, and Asia this is Keon," Skye greeted.

"Hello, it's nice to finally meet you. I've seen you around and always wanted to holla, but you always have a man in your face," Keon said to Asia with a wink.

Asia forcefully grabbed his hand looking for a wedding band. When she didn't see one, she pulled him closer to her. "Well, I damn sure have never seen you before. Nice to meet you, too, boo," she said grinning.

Skye shook her head then smiled. Asia was certainly over the top, with a huge personality, but she loved her no less.

The three sat talking as Asia and Keon flirted back and forth with each other. Moments later, Asia excused herself to use the bathroom.

Keon grabbed Skye's hand mimicking Asia, "nice to meet you, too, boo. Your friend is something else," he teased.

They both laughed. "Yes, she is," Skye replied.

"So Skye, how did a nice, beautiful woman like you end up with a man like Sandino Washington?"

"What are you talking about?"

"You know what I'm talking about," Keon answered.

Skye looked at him funny. "A man like…"

7

Skye stopped in mid-sentence with a frightening expression on her face when she saw Sandino staring at her through the window. His eyes were cold as he walked toward the door at a rapid pace.

Little did Skye know, Sandino had become angry after walking around for the past thirty minutes looking for her. Now, to find her up in another man's face was a no-no, especially since he hadn't invited Keon in the first place.

"Oh my God. Keon, please leave now," Skye damn near begged. "He's coming." It felt as if she was about to pass out.

Chapter Two

Sandino burst through the door eyeballing his new trainer. He looked like a pit bull ready to attack. "Nigga, what the fuck you doing all up on my wife?"

Everyone knew Skye was his prized possession, and that Sandino was extremely jealous. However, Keon obviously hadn't gotten the memo.

"Sandino man, it's not like that," Keon said moving away.

Without hesitation, Skye jumped up and ran toward her husband. She grabbed his hand and gently massaged it.

"Baby, let's not fight tonight, we were just talking," she pleaded. "Besides, we have guests."

Sandino yanked his hand away and grabbed her by the arm. "Oh, so you must wanna fuck 'em since you tryna take up for this nigga!"

Skye frantically shook her head. "No, of course not. Baby, please don't do this."

Seconds later, Cruze came running in the kitchen. "Come on Sandino, let's take a walk outside."

Sandino let go of Skye's arm, but still hadn't calmed down. "Naw fuck that Cruze, this nigga tryna play me!" he shouted then staggered back and forth.

"Look, I'll handle him later Sandino, you've had too much to drink. Let's chill and enjoy the rest of the night. Your wife went through a lot of trouble to prepare this party for you," Cruze responded.

Cruze knew his friend was about to explode at any minute. He was trying his best to calm him down, but he also didn't know how much longer he could deal with Sandino's abusive behavior. His friend had gotten way out of control lately.

Suddenly, Sandino jumped back in Keon's face. "Muthafucka, I did my research on you. I know your track record; how you got the last player's wife pregnant. Not to mention I heard you damn near stalk all the NFL wives. Well, that shit ain't goin' down ova here!" Sandino was so close to Keon, he was now spitting in his face.

"Sandino, that's some bullshit, I would never disrespect you or any other player like that," Keon replied. "I've worked too hard for my reputation to be on the line."

"Oh yeah, well fuck you and your reputation," Sandino shot back.

Asia quickly ran out the bathroom when she heard the commotion. "Sandino, Keon and I were the ones talking about going on a date. Skye was just keeping him company while I used the restroom," she said, trying to come to her friend's defense.

"Was I talkin' to your hot-ass, Asia?" Sandino questioned with an attitude. "Keon, you fired. I only agreed to let you train me because you came highly recommended, but nobody fuckin' disrespects me!" Sandino yelled. He then grabbed Skye by the arm again, pulling her through the house.

"Sandino, chill the fuck out!" Cruze yelled running behind him.

Ignoring his friend, it wasn't long before Sandino started flipping out on all the other guests at the party. Skye was so humiliated as Sandino's anger increased by the second.

"All you muthafuckas get the hell out my house now!" Sandino roared. Knowing his boys would get everyone out, he pushed Skye up the stairs toward their bedroom

"Sandino, you promised you wouldn't hit me again!" Skye screamed after he closed the door then pushed her onto the bed.

"Well, bitch I lied," Sandino replied before applying a massive blow across her face. "I told your monkey ass about walkin' around here flirtin' wit' every man you see, didn't I?"

Her light Alicia Keys type complexion instantly turned red.

"Sandino please, the boys will hear you," Skye pleaded with tears in her eyes.

"So, my son's are too soft as it is, always under your fuckin' ass. They need to know the man is in charge!" When Sandino threw a quick jab, Skye quickly turned her head trying to protect her face.

"You tryin' to resist bitch?" he asked angrily.

At that moment, Sandino grabbed a wad of Skye's hair sending her body to the floor. Seconds later, he jumped on top of her, then landed several more punches to her face before grabbing Skye's neck. When she noticed the white residue inside Sandino's nostrils and his dilated pupils, Skye wondered how many pills he'd crushed and sniffed this time. She also wondered if he was abusing more than just pain killers. Although she considered herself a fighter, Skye was no match for Sandino's huge muscular frame. She'd learned over the years that if she didn't fight back the beatings were less severe.

He unzipped his pants and leaned over her. "Open your mouth bitch!"

When Skye refused, he kicked her in the stomach causing her to scream. As soon as her mouth flew open, Sandino pulled out his dick and started urinating in her mouth and all over her face.

"That'll teach yo' ass not to ever disrespect me!"

Skye began to sob and tried not to gag from the smell of the urine that irritated the open wounds on her face. A few seconds later, Sandino reached between her legs and ripped off her panties. He then pushed her legs back toward her neck and entered her forcefully with his now stiff dick. As he pounded and pounded her pussy, it felt like he was purposely trying to puncture her uterus. When Skye screamed out in agonizing pain, he put his hands around her neck again.

"Shut up! This my pussy, and don't ever forget that shit. I'll kill everybody in this fuckin' house if you keep pissin' me off!" he yelled with each vicious stroke.

A sudden knock at the door only escalated his erratic behavior. However, when the knocks continued, Sandino finally decided to release the grip around her neck. "Skye, you better not say one fuckin' word," he demanded before pulling out of her.

Skye instantly started coughing uncontrollably as Sandino jumped up and pulled up his pants.

"Who the fuck knockin' on my damn door?" he yelled.

"Is everything alright Sandino? I just wanted to apologize," Keon said.

"Nigga, you got a lot of fuckin' balls right now. Matter fact why are you still here?" Sandino grabbed his .45 out of the night stand drawer and snatched open the bedroom door.

Skye listened to what sounded like a scuffle in the hallway between Sandino and Keon which was soon followed by shots and footsteps running down the stairs. Skye laid on the bedroom floor bloody and bruised as Sandino yelled downstairs at the few people still left at the party. She then heard Cruze trying to plead with his friend to give him the gun and calm down.

"Get the fuck out my house now!" Sandino demanded putting everyone including his boys out once and for all.

A few minutes later she heard Sandino set the alarm. Within moments, he walked back into their bedroom slamming the door behind him. He jumped back on top of her and finished right where he left off, only this time his bi-polar behavior actually apologized and tried to make excuses for beating her.

With the amount of alcohol and drugs that Sandino had consumed, Skye knew it was only a matter of time before he passed out. She looked over at his gun sitting on the night stand and thought about grabbing it. She wanted desperately to blow his fucking brains out, but just like all the other times she'd planned to kill him, she would think of the prison time and her kids being left without a mother, then change her mind. She knew her only way out was to leave him.

"And I'm damn sure not leaving empty handed. I'll make sure of that," she said to herself.

🙶🙶🙶🙶🙶🙶🙶🙶

Skye lay motionless listening to Sandino's breathing to make absolutely sure he was in a deep sleep before she crawled out of bed at exactly two a.m. Her entire body was covered with urine and blood from the injuries she sustained from his latest tirade. With her left eye swollen shut and her ribs feeling as if they were broken, Skye knew this was it. She couldn't do it anymore. The sympathy she once felt for Sandino being abused as a child, his bouts with depression and having suicidal thoughts were gone. She now wished he'd done her a favor and actually ended his life during the last suicidal overdose attempt.

When Skye glanced over on the night stand for his gun, it was gone. She wanted to grab it for protection during her escape, but obviously Sandino was two steps ahead of her.

Damn, he must've moved it before he fell asleep, she thought.

Seconds later, Skye decided it was time to make her move. Her heart raced as she slowly slid out of bed then crawled on all fours until she reached the door. She didn't have on any clothes and was scared to ramble in the room looking for some, so she grabbed the white dress she wore at the party off the floor. It was bloody and ripped, but she didn't care. All she wanted to do was get her kids and leave.

Skye glanced over at Sandino once more to make sure was he still in the same position. After verifying that he hadn't moved, she stood up, opened the bedroom door and quietly closed it behind her. She slid on the dress and ran down the hall bare footed. She almost jumped out of her skin when she bumped into Ms. Petra who was standing in the hallway with Payton in her arms. Ms. Petra peeped down the hall in the direction of their bedroom before speaking.

"Oh me dear child, look at you beautiful face. Dat monster does not deserve such a wonderful family. Take de children and run…go! Me have bags packed for all of you; me spirit told me tonight you leave him. Get de boys. Jordan fell asleep in Kareem's room. I will watch for dat blood clot demon," she whispered in her deep Jamaican accent. The two of them had discussed Skye's getaway several times.

"Thank you Ms. Petra. I don't know what…"

"Sssshhh," Ms. Petra said then looked down the hall once again. "Hush chile before he hears us. Go get da boys. I'll meet you downstairs."

When Skye ran to Kareem's room, she didn't waste much time waking both of her son's up. Luckily, the T.V. and Kareem's desk lamp was on, so they didn't have to move around in the dark.

"Ma, what happened? Did he hit you again?" Jordan asked once he noticed his mother's face.

"Shhhh, I'm okay we have to go now," Skye said. "Put your shoes on." As soon as Skye realized that Kareem hadn't bulged, she looked at him with a pleading set of eyes. "Come on Kareem, I know you love your dad, but we can't stay." When Kareem still didn't move, tears started to stream down Skye's face. "Kareem please, I don't wanna leave without you. You know if I stay he's gonna eventually kill me. Look at what happened tonight. Can't you see…things have gotten out of control?" Skye knew how stubborn her sixteen year old son could be, and hoped he would see her point.

Seeing his mother cry put an instant soft spot in his heart. Never saying a word, Kareem only nodded his head before grabbing his favorite pair of Jordan tennis shoes then followed his mother out the door.

Skye motioned for them to 'hurry up' as her heart began to beat profusely. They tip-toed down the hall on the expensive marble floors stepping over the debris Sandino left from the recent shooting. They all couldn't help but notice several bullet holes in the wall as they walked down the spiral staircase and toward the foyer. The fact that the house was so quiet, made Skye extremely nervous.

When they approached Ms. Petra, she passed Skye her cell phone.

"Here, I found ya cell on da kitchen floor. If you lose me number call my brotha's restaurant Island Grill in Kingston Jamaica, he'll reach me. Be safe and never look back," Ms. Petra whispered passing her the baby.

The two embraced with a hug. Ms. Petra then reached over and hugged the boys. She looked at Kareem.

"Kareem, you da oldest born, protect you mom, she need you!" Ms. Petra pushed him toward Skye. "You go now!"

For a moment, Skye briefly had second thoughts about leaving the lifestyle she'd become so accustomed to, but knew this was her only chance. After safely reaching the front door, she glanced back at Ms. Petra who signaled for them to go while she kept as eye out for Sandino. Kareem kept looking back wishing they didn't have to leave, but knew his place was with his mother.

Skye quickly punched in the code on the alarm system, motioned for Kareem and Jordan to grab the bags then eased the front door open. After running across the expensive landscaping and passing Ms. Petra's dented up Mazda 626, they all headed toward Skye's new Jaguar XJ in the driveway.

Skye's entire body ached, but her desire to get away and provide a safe environment for herself and her kids was far more important, so she blocked out the discomfort and agonizing pain.

Feeling paranoid, she surveyed the block making sure none of Sandino's boys were parked down the street watching the house as they did on occasions. After making sure the coast was clear, she reached under the rock in the front yard that said, "The Washington's" and grabbed the spare key she'd hidden for emergencies.

Skye hit the key remote and when it chirped, she quickly opened the car door and put the baby in her car seat and watched as her sons tossed the bags in the car. She was just about to get in when she saw Ms. Petra running full speed out of the house.

"He's coming, get in de car and go!"

Skye's eyelids widened with fear when she saw Sandino running toward them. Frantically, she jumped in the car, closed and locked the doors and then put the key in the ignition. She prayed that Sandino's love for his kids would keep him from spraying her car with bullets.

"Ma, hurry up!" Jordan yelled.

As soon as Skye put the car in reverse, they heard a loud thump. Her heart skipped a beat when she realized that Sandino had already managed to leap on the hood of the car. Skye understood now why they'd nick named him Sandino, 'Fast as Lighting' Washington on the football field.

"Skye, get your ass out the fuckin' car now!" he yelled looking at her through the front windshield. "You're not takin' my kids away from me!" His eyes were blood shot red as he began to pound on the glass.

Seeing him on top of the hood in his underwear gave Skye a sense of relief that he didn't have time to grab his gun.

"You think you can just leave me? I will hunt your ass down!" Sandino continued to yell. By this point, Payton started to scream as well. "Open the door for your father, Kareem!" Sandino shouted toward the back seat.

Fear that his father would beat him next, Kareem extended his hand. But by the time his hand reached the door handle, Skye hit the gas and backed out of the driveway causing her husband to fall onto the ground. She slammed her foot on the accelerator skidding down the street with Sandino yelling like a mad man. Skye looked around wondering where the nosey neighbors were now when she really needed them.

Her son's watched their father's adrenalin kick in as he tried to run behind the car, but soon stopped, unable to keep up. Skye hit speeds as high as 80 mph as soon as they made it out of the neighborhood and onto the highway.

"Where are we going?" Jordan asked.

"I'm not sure, but say goodbye to Florida," Skye said nervously looking in her rear view mirror.

Kareem was distraught. "We're leaving Florida? No!"

"He'll hunt us down if we stay here!" Skye fired back.

It looked like both of her boys wanted to cry.

Skye was relived when she looked at the gas needle and saw a full tank of gas. The one positive thing that Sandino ever did was keep her car on full. Headed toward I-95 North she quickly thought, *you've seen the last of your family Sandino Washington.*

Jackie D.

Chapter Three

After driving for almost six hours Skye finally grabbed some baby wipes out Payton's bag and attempted to get rid of the urine smell from her body. Out of all the things Sandino had done over the years, he'd never violated her like that. Treating her like a toilet was definitely the last straw.

As she watched the sun come up, Skye breathed a sigh of relief. "I finally did it. I'm free," she said to herself. "He can never hurt us now."

Shaking her head, it still hurt knowing their marriage was over after all she'd done to keep it together. However, as soon as Skye thought about her sanity and piece of mind, she was able to force a slight smile. Not to mention, as long as her children were safe, nothing else mattered.

The more Skye continued to drive, her eyes started to become heavy. She didn't even realize that the car began to drift until she heard a horn blowing. Suddenly, Skye jerked the wheel back, just before running off the road. Her heart started to pound once again.

"Oh my God," Skye said, just before pulling over. She then glanced in the back seat at her kids who were still fast asleep.

Exhausted, she looked over to her right and saw a sign that read restaurants and gas. Deciding that Jacksonville was far enough away for them to stop, she put her blinker on and took the exit. She knew the kids were probably ready for some food, and Payton definitely needed changing. As soon as Skye stopped to make a right turn, Jordan woke up yawning and dazed. Moments later, he reached over the seat and kissed Skye on the cheek.

"I'm proud of you mom. You got out before it was too late," he said. He was so mature for a fourteen year old.

Skye looked at her son and smiled. It made her feel good to hear him say that. A part of her felt guilty about dragging them away from the only home they'd ever known.

After riding around for a few minutes, the only place open was a small diner. Once Skye pulled in the parking lot, she woke Kareem up, who hadn't said two words since they left. He was close to his father and she worried about what kind of impact leaving might have on him. She grabbed her suitcase.

"Let's go freshen up in the bathroom and then get something to eat," Skye said before anxiously looking around the parking lot.

Even though they were three hundred and forty miles away, she still had to make sure Sandino wasn't anywhere to be found.

Both Kareem and Jordan seemed sluggish and hesitant.

She looked at her watch. "Its 8:00 a.m., this is the time you hungry guys eat anyway, so come on. Grab Payton's car seat."

Once inside Skye stopped and scanned the place as if she didn't belong. It was clean, but very old fashioned. All the tables were covered with checkered table cloths and dusty fake flowers as an old Elvis Presley song played from the juke box in the corner. The red-neck looking truck drivers eating watched them closely as they made their way toward the bathroom. Skye even noticed a huge red headed man also staring at them from the kitchen. At that moment Skye realized she was still wearing the torn bloody white dress not to mention her badly bruised face. She could only imagine what they were thinking. She grabbed her Gucci sunglasses and quickly put them on, like that made a difference.

After all of them squeezed into the one stall bathroom and locked the door, Skye pulled her shoulder length hair up into a ponytail then quickly changed into her Juicy Couture sweat suit. However, she refused to look in the mirror afraid of what her face looked like this time. Instead she changed the baby's diaper and waited for the boys to finish before they all exited together. They ignored the stares again then sat in a booth near the door and grabbed three menus. Skye however could barely make out the words due to her swollen eyes. Not only was she in pain, but she needed rest and couldn't wait until she could get a good night's sleep.

Minutes later, the waitress appeared from the back with her pad and pen ready to take their orders.

"Hello, what can I get y'all this morning?" she asked in a cheerful, deep country voice. Her eyebrows frowned at the sight of Skye's face. "Oh my God, are you alright darling?"

"Yes, I'm fine. Can you please just take our order? My boys are starving," Skye replied.

"We want pancakes, bacon and orange juice," Jordan said.

"We have a meal called the Ultimate Breakfast that includes all of that for only $4.99, it'll be much cheaper. Would you like that?" the waitress asked looking at Skye.

"Look lady, the price isn't an issue," Skye said with an attitude.

"Oh…I didn't mean to offend you. It's just that I have two boys at home around their age and I know how much they can eat. The Ultimate Breakfast is what they usually get."

Skye changed her tone realizing the lady was only being nice. "Three Ultimate Breakfasts, with orange juice will be fine," Skye replied.

"Okay, I'll be right back," the woman said walking

away. She returned shortly with the same cheerful smile. "Here are your drinks, let me know if you need anything. My name is Kim and that's my big handsome husband working back there in the kitchen Jim, we're the owners. Your food will be out in a minute," she added before walking away again.

"Jim and Kim? You've got to be kidding me," Skye said to herself.

As she placed a straw in her glass, she looked down at her watch realizing that it was a few minutes after eight. Normally, she would've still been in bed while Ms. Petra attended to Payton. Now, she was on the run with nowhere to go. Skye knew leaving Sandino was the best idea, but she was definitely gonna miss the live-in help.

How quickly shit can change, Skye thought to herself as she continued to glance out the window. Even though they were in another city, she just didn't trust Sandino.

Then suddenly out of nowhere Kareem finally spoke. "I stole daddy's key to his gun closet and I got one of his guns out when I heard him beating you, but Ms. Petra caught me. She made me put the gun back," he said with a strange look on his face.

Kareem reminded Skye so much of Sandino, especially with his quick temper. Even though he'd inherited her fair skin tone, and a mole under his lip, his mannerism seemed to be identical to his father.

Skye's face revealed a shocked expression. She knew her boys were getting older and she could no longer hide the abuse from them.

"Thanks for having my back Kareem. I know how hard it's been for you. Your dad has a problem and until he gets some help, I just can't allow him to be around y'all. Things will be okay though. We'll settle down in a nice city and you boys can make new friends and have fun for a change. Playing sports is your choice from now on."

"Are we gonna be poor?" Jordan asked.

"No, we'll be fine," Skye tried to assure.

After all the ass beatings she received over the years, Skye made sure she'd stashed something away for this rainy day.

When Skye glanced out the window again, her eyes widened when she saw a thin, skinny, white man looking at her car. He even walked around to each side peeping in the windows. She felt uneasy wondering if Sandino sent him. She watched until he came inside, spoke to several of the truck drivers then headed to the kitchen and put on an apron.

"He must work here," she said to herself noticing he had red hair just like the owner Jim. "I wonder if his damn name is Tim," she joked to herself.

A few minutes later, he walked back out the kitchen and over to the table with their food. "Hello, is that your car?" he asked placing all three plates down.

Unsure about whether to answer him Skye paused before speaking. "Yes it is, why?"

"I'm just asking cause that's a mighty nice vehicle you got there," he stated in a southern tone. "I want to get me a car like that one day, been saving my money working here with my mom and pop. I got me a 1999 Honda Accord with some ten inch rims." Skye let out a huge sigh hoping he would get the hint and leave, especially since their food had arrived, but he kept right on talking. "I just got it painted and tint put on the windows. That's my baby. It's parked in the back." He stood there for a few seconds like he wanted Skye to respond. "Can I get you anything else?"

"No," Skye quickly said before putting a piece of bacon in her mouth.

"Well, nice talking to you," he finally said then walked away.

Skye shook her head as a million thoughts seemed to suddenly fight for her attention. She knew the guy was only trying to be nice, but with all the drama she had going on right now, there was no way she could listen to anyone else's problems. Suddenly, she started thinking about her and Sandino's early days, before the fame, the drugs and the abuse; days when they used to have fun; days when they latched onto each other and talked about both of their horrible childhoods.

Sandino grew up in West Baltimore's oldest and worst housing projects, called Lexington Terrace with his prostitute mother Peaches. He watched her turn tricks and get abused everyday by her pimp, Hollywood, who was also Sandino's father. Even though Skye wasn't considered a project chick, and grew up in the Prince George's County area, her circumstances were just as bad. At the age of ten, both of her parents were killed in a car accident, forcing Skye to live in foster homes when neither of her aunts would take her in. She ended up going from one home to the next with two outfits in her possession, but somehow still managed to keep straight A's all throughout school. Her living arrangements didn't seem to get any better until she received a full scholarship to college, and moved onto campus. Those same aunts had the nerve to try to come into her life years later when they found out she was married to a professional ball player.

When she married Sandino he promised to love and protect her. Skye never imagined in her wildest dreams she would become a victim of domestic abuse. Thinking back on it, Skye now knew she should've left him the very first time he put his hands on her. But at the time she just wasn't strong enough to walk away.

But I am now? I have to be, I must protect my sons from picking up their father's wicked ways, she thought.

Suddenly, Skye felt herself about to break down so she jumped up and told the boys she would be right back and went into the bathroom. She couldn't let her boys see her like this.

Tears were racing down her face as soon as she hit the door. Needing to let it all out, she fell back against the sink and released a horrifying scream. Skye knew that everyone in the diner probably heard her cries but she'd held in the pain long enough. A few seconds later the waitress Kim burst into the restroom.

"Are you okay darling?" she asked with concern.

Skye grabbed a paper towel and wiped her face then looked at the woman. "Does it look like I'm okay? No I'm not okay! My husband has been abusing me for years, and last night I finally left him. I don't know where the fuck I'm going. I left a million dollar home to live on the run. My kids deserve a home!" Skye yelled as she broke down crying again.

It didn't take long for the waitress to give Skye a consoling hug. "What your kids really deserve is you, their mother and by the look of your face, if you hadn't left when you did, he would've killed you."

Skye didn't respond.

"I didn't mean to get in your business earlier, but my sister was once in an abusive relationship. And if it wasn't for the help she received from different people along the way, she wouldn't be here today. She owns a Bed and Breakfast in Georgia now. I'm not sure which way you're headed, but if you need a safe place to stay I can call and tell her you and the kids might be stopping by. There are people out here to help you, just let me know if you're interested," Kim said. She rubbed Skye across her back a few more times. "Now, I'll give you some time alone."

Once Kim closed the door, Skye got herself together before finally deciding to look into the mirror. What stared back at her was a woman with not only a bruised and swollen reflection, but also a broken spirit. She was miles away from Sandino, but he still seemed to have a hold on her. Controlling her mind, bringing her down and making her think she couldn't make it without him. To make matters worse, she was also confused. When the three-carat diamond earrings sparkling in her ears reminded her of happier days, she wished Sandino could go to rehab and get some help so they could stay together. But on the other hand, Skye knew he would never change, so she had to move on and make a better life for them without him.

Skye realized now she had to become her old self in order to be there for her children. With a sudden survival mode etched in her mind, she splashed some cold water on her face then gave herself a little pep talk before returning back to the table.

While the boys continued to eat, Skye smiled at Payton who sat quietly in her car seat, until she suddenly remembered to contact Asia. When Sandino broke her arm a year ago, Skye was finally fed up and secretly started planning her escape. It was at that moment when she began withdrawing money out of her and Sandino's joint account and depositing it into an account under Asia's name at the bank where she worked. The only downfall was, Skye knew she hadn't taken enough to last her very long, but it would just have to do.

She grabbed her cell phone and sent Asia a text message with only three words.

We escaped safely.

A few minutes later Skye's phone vibrated. It was Asia.

Finally, r u all ok? I was so worried. I was the one who sent Keon upstairs to knock on the door. We had to stop him from beating u.

I'm ok. Bruised but free of his ass. Thx for having my back. Keon is nice, but keep our situation a secret. We can't trust nobody! I need the cash. I'll contact you when I get settled, Skye replied.

I got u, it's our secret. I'll send cash as soon I hear from u. I love u, please be careful, Asia text back.

Ok we will, Skye responded.

When Skye felt another message coming through, she instantly assumed it was Asia texting back. She clicked on the message and read it.

Hope u enjoyin ur meal in that dump. Did u really

think I would let u get away that easy? I put a trackin device on ur car the day I bought it. Now bring ur monkey ass outside quietly before I come in and shoot that muthafucka up!

Chapter Four 🏈

Skye's eyes widened as she looked out the window and saw Sandino's snow white Mercedes S550 in the parking lot. She then dropped the phone, frantic with fear when she saw him getting out of the car along with Cruze and Black.

"Ma, what's wrong?" Kareem asked noticing her behavior.

"He found us," Skye managed to say.

Both the boys instantly looked out the window.

"How did he find us?" Jordan questioned.

"Come on, get the bags…let's go," Skye said thinking fast. Grabbing Payton's seat, she quickly ran toward the kitchen. When she saw the young guy who talked to her about her car, Skye got his attention. "Listen I really need your help. I just left my abusive husband and now he's outside threatening to kill me. Please…we have to get out of here, before he comes inside. Can you please trade cars with me?" Skye frantically asked.

The young guy looked at her like she was crazy. "Are you serious?"

Skye looked back to see if Sandino had come inside. "Yes, I am. Please hurry."

The guy seemed hesitant at first before saying, "Come this way." He led them through the kitchen and out the back door. It wasn't long before they exchanged keys and he helped them get inside his car. Seconds later, Kim ran outside and came over to the car holding a piece of paper.

"Here's my sister's number and address. Trust me, she can help."

"Thanks so much," Skye said, as tears rolled down her face. She was embarrassed about the way she'd acted toward them earlier.

"See that road right there?" the young guy pointed. "It's a back road that will lead you straight to the interstate. Take that one. I doubt if he will."

"We'll even try and stall him if he comes in," Kim added.

"Thanks again," Skye replied before pulling off in the beat-up Honda.

Just as she drove off, Sandino and his boys entered the diner looking around for her and the kids. After quickly telling Black to check the bathroom, Sandino looked around and showcased his discuss.

"I can't believe that bitch had my boys eating in here." He grabbed a napkin off the table and wiped his hands as if the place made them dirty.

A few seconds later Black came out the restroom with Skye's bloody dress. "She's not in the restroom, but I found this in the trash can."

Sandino started pacing the floor. "Skye get your ass out here, now!" he yelled toward the kitchen.

When he didn't get a response he signaled for Cruze to check things out. Cruze attempted to head toward the back, but was caught by surprise when Jim stood in the kitchen pointing a shot gun directly at his chest.

"Don't move or I'll shoot," he yelled. Cruze instantly put his hands up as Jim backed him into the dining area. "Look boys, we don't want any trouble around here so I think its best y'all get on outta here!"

When Sandino looked like he was reaching in his coat

pocket, Jim cocked his gun then pointed it deeper into Cruze's chest.

"I've already called the law so unless you boys want to spend the night in jail and get them fancy clothes all dirtied up, I suggest you turn around and head back out that door. The young lady you looking for ain't here anymore," Jim stated.

I know I can take this old muthafucka out, Sandino thought. He wanted to reach for his gun so bad, his hand started to twitch.

As soon as Cruze saw Sandino's facial expression, he already knew that his life was possibly in jeopardy. Thinking fast, he elbowed Jim and dove to the floor. It was at that moment when Sandino pulled out and fired a shot. Jim however, quickly fired back by shooting a round in the air. Both Black and Sandino knew their fire power couldn't compete with the shot gun, so they quickly made their way out the door and ran to the car.

"What about Cruze?" Black shouted.

"That nigga on his own," Sandino returned after jumping into the car.

By the time Black looked back in the direction of the diner, he saw Cruze running out like a track star. "Come on, nigga!" he shouted.

When the car pulled up, Cruze jumped inside like Bo from the *Dukes of Hazard* just as Sandino skidded out of the parking lot. Breathing heavily, he was mad as hell as thoughts of Sandino possibly leaving him behind entered his mind. Knowing he had his own Glock 17, Cruze wanted to pull his shit out and teach Sandino a thing or two about loyalty, but the thought of prison promptly erased that idea. When Black kept laughing and cracking jokes like the shit was funny, Cruze instantly started yelling.

"Sandino what the fuck were you thinkin'? That man had a fuckin' 12 gage pointed at my chest and you still tried to reach for your damn gun. He could've killed me, and then y'all niggas had the nerve to try and leave me in that muthafucka!"

"Nigga, stop fuckin' cryin' like a lil' bitch! You made it to the car didn't you? That hill billy muthafucka won't gon shoot you," Sandino said with a smirk.

"You don't know that shit," Cruze fired back.

"Trust me, he didn't want that heat," Sandino replied.

Suddenly, he slammed on the breaks and put the car in reverse.

"What the fuck are you doing?" Black asked when he realized Sandino was headed back to the diner.

Sandino ignored his friend before pulling up next to Skye's Jaguar. Seconds later, he shot several rounds into the car then drove back off.

"That bitch won't be so lucky next time!"

$$\textbf{\textit{ØØØØØØØØ}}$$

Sandino drove recklessly down the highway with Rick Ross singing, "I think I'm Big Meech, Larry Hover, whipping work, halleluiah."

He was mad as hell that Skye had somehow managed to slip away. At one point he wondered if she was still hiding inside the diner and the people were just covering for her. But he also knew that Payton feared loud noises and with all the yelling and gun shots going on, she definitely would've started crying.

"How do you think she got out?" Black curiously asked.

"I have no idea. That bitch had to go out the back or something," Sandino replied.

Black still seemed puzzled. "What about her car? There's no way she could've walked."

Thinking about how Skye managed to avoid him or who could've helped her, made Sandino bang the steering wheel with his fist. He had to find her; she was his property…had been that way since college. No other man would ever have her as long as he was living on this earth.

Sandino dialed her cell phone hoping she picked up. When it went straight to voicemail, he became enraged all over again. He waited for the beep and yelled over the music leaving a message.

"Skye you playin' wit' fire baby. To muthafuckin' death do us part you can believe that shit!"

When Sandino hung up, he reached in his shirt pocket and pulled out three Oxycontin pills, threw them in his mouth and swallowed. "I wish I could crush these for a better high," he mumbled to himself. "Better yet, I could use somethin' stronger."

Sandino was in such a zone he forgot all about his boys even being in the car with him until Black spoke up.

"You alright man?" he asked.

Sandino turned the music down. "Hell no I ain't alright. After all I do for that bitch and this is how she tryna repay me? I give her everything. I might slap her ass around every now and then, but she be deservin' that shit."

"Man, she's probably just pissed because you embarrassed her ass at the party. She'll be back though, shit rough out here. She won't be able to survive without any paper. Skye likes to spend money; she'll lose her mind not being able to run back and forth getting dough out of y'all bank like she usually does," Black lectured.

"What the fuck you talkin' 'bout Black?" Sandino questioned.

"You told me to watch her every move and that's what she been doing for the past two months. She go get dough out y'all bank and then go meet that bitch Asia at the bank where she works. Then she goes shopping, taking all damn day," Black replied.

Sandino was quiet for a minute.

What reason would Skye have to keep goin' to the bank, he thought. *She has an Amex black card and access to the cash in the house to go shoppin' wit'. My account did look a little light the last time I checked, but I thought it was all the crazy spendin' for my habit and trickin' these bitches. Somethin' don't fuckin' sound right. I'm about to go holla at Asia. I never liked the connivin' bitch and if I find out she helped Skye steal some of my money, that bitch is goin' down,* Sandino thought to himself.

Cruze hadn't said anything the entire ride back to Miami. Still pissed at Sandino for leaving him, he didn't bother to tell his friend that he was wasting his time calling Skye's phone. When he dove onto the diner floor, Cruze noticed her phone along with her loose battery underneath a booth. He recognized it by the Swarovski crystal Miami Dolphins case she had custom made just three weeks earlier. Now, with Sandino's loyalty in question, not only was he keeping the information to himself, but Cruze hoped he never found Skye.

She deserves better anyway, he thought.

Chapter Five 🏈

Sandino pulled up at the bank where Asia worked at exactly 3:15 p.m. It normally took anybody doing a normal rate of speed almost six hours to drive from Jacksonville, but in this case it only took Sandino five. Driving well over eighty-five miles per hour the entire trip, all he could think about was how Asia probably helped his wife double cross him, which was way out of line.

As soon as he saw her black metallic Hummer H3 with the personalized Texas plates sitting out front, he couldn't wait to confront her. He also wondered why Skye hung around her country-ass in the first place. In his mind Asia was no where near on his wife's level, and nothing like the other NFL wives Skye should've been hanging out with.

"You might wanna leave the heat here. You don't want muthafuckas to think a Miami Dolphin player is trying to rob the joint," Black joked.

Sandino had to smile. "Oh, yeah you right." He removed the .45 from his waist then placed it underneath the seat. "Cruze, you alright back there?" Sandino asked. "You ain't said two words since we left. Don't tell me your ass still salty."

Cruze bit his bottom lip to keep from flipping out. "No, I'm straight."

"You sure nigga? If you got something to get off yo'

chest, speak up," Sandino added.

Cruze looked at Black's tar colored skin as he laughed at Sandino's response.

"Why the fuck is your flunky-ass laughing?" Cruze questioned.

"Because I want to, nigga," Black fired back.

Just as the two men were about to get into a shouting match, Sandino spoke up. "Look, Cruze yo' beef is wit' me. Now, do you have somethin' to say to me?"

"I said I'm straight," Cruze replied.

"Good. 'Cause I don't need no bitch-ass dudes around." Sandino looked at both men, then said, "I'll be right back."

When he entered the bank, Sandino walked right over to Asia who was standing with a customer. "Asia, can I speak to you for a minute?" He couldn't help but notice the way her ass poked out of her tight fitting pin striped suit.

She shot her eyes in his direction. "Have a seat, I'll be right with you sir," Asia said in a professional tone.

"I need to speak to you now, bitch!" Sandino responded loud enough for the people in the bank to hear.

Asia was beyond embarrassed. "Please excuse me for a minute," she said to her customer. She escorted Sandino to her small glass office off to the side. "Sandino, don't be coming to my job disrespecting me. I'm not Skye," she stated. "Besides...why are you even here? This shit better be good."

"So, what's your job title around here?"

Asia seemed confused. "Branch Manager, why?"

"Just wondering why my wife fucked wit' such a low class bitch such as yourself. I'm also wonderin' if I should get your ass fired or just fuck you up myself."

Asia's eyes widened. "What the hell is your crazy-ass talking about? Don't come up in here with that Ike Turner shit."

"Do you know where Skye and my kids are?" he asked.

"Skye left you?" Asia asked trying to sound convincing.

"You know she did Asia, don't' fuckin' play wit' me."

"I haven't seen Skye since the party. I've been calling her all day, but she won't pick up the phone."

"Look, you can stop that innocent role playin' shit. I also know you helped her steal some of my fuckin' money! I got a good idea that she's been makin' withdrawals from our account and then bringin' money ova here. But let's hope that's not true."

"Really…and how can you be so sure?"

"Trust me, I got eyes everywhere."

Asia stared at him for a few seconds. "I thought you wanted her gone."

"Who the hell ever told you that?" Sandino questioned.

"Well, I thought after fucking me all those times, there was no way you would've wanted to stay."

Sandino looked around to make sure no one was trying to eavesdrop. His infidelity was nobody's business. "Bitch, stop talkin' that dumb shit. I told you ova and ova that you were just another piece of ass to me, nothin' more."

Asia's ghetto demeanor finally appeared. "Oh, really. Well, maybe that's why I helped her then."

Instantly, Sandino stepped up to Asia like a boxer before a fight. He wanted so badly to slap the shit out of her for being bold all of a sudden.

"Asia, let me just say this…if you been transferrin' my shit, then you better fuckin' transfer it back, because if you don't, I suggest you watch yo' back. I know where you live," Sandino threatened then grabbed her up by the collar.

Asia pulled away. "Sandino, you better get the fuck out my office before I call security."

Sandino laughed. "I don't give a fuck about no damn fake-ass security. You're gonna need more than that to keep me off your ass if I find out that you helped Skye."

As soon as he walked out, Sandino thought to himself, *and here I was tellin' Skye not to trust that bitch. Guess I should'a took my own advice.*

PPPPPPPP

After dropping his boys off, Sandino rode around for hours getting high. Not wanting to go home to his empty house, he pulled up at his favorite massage parlor, The Zhen Spa. It was located in a secluded private area on the out skirts of Miami. From the outside it looked like a rundown warehouse, but the inside was truly paradise.

He noticed the small number of cars in the parking lot as he stepped out of his car, then glanced at his new chrome 19' inch, Asanti rims.

"Damn they look good," he said, walking toward the building.

Once inside, the small lobby area was decorated with Asian inspired pieces and Shoji screens on each side. It was also equipped with video cameras in every corner of the ceilings which made Sandino feel uneasy every time he waited to be buzzed in.

As soon as someone buzzed him inside, Sandino walked down the narrow corridor with pastel colored walls like he owned the place until he reached two large wooden double doors. However, when he tried to enter, a large muscular man dressed in all black quickly stopped him.

"Hold up, I know you not tryna play me muthafucka. After all the money me and my niggas have spent up in this joint. Shit, we probably pay your damn salary!" Sandino yelled. He hated wanna be work-out type niggas that always had something to prove. "Where the hell is Sora?" Sandino asked.

The man frowned, stepped inside the door and yelled. "Sora!"

A few minutes later Sora appeared in the door way. You couldn't wipe the smile off her face as she ran and jumped up in Sandino's arms then kissed him in the mouth.

"Sandino, my baby, it been long time. Why you not come see Sora? Used to come see me two, three times a week, now no show for long time. You don't love Sora no more?" she asked in a heavy Asian accent.

Sora was a petite native from Taiwan who loved to show off her large breast implants that Sandino was responsible for. They stood out like sore thumbs on her tiny frame.

"I been busy Sora, handling business. You know you're my favorite girl."

Sora started smiling. She loved Sandino, and somehow believed that he was going to marry her so she could become a legal citizen.

"I want you and another bitch," Sandino stated.

"Okay, we have great new Vietnamese, Thai and Taiwan girls, but no more Hong Kong girls," she said apologetically.

Sandino thought, *shit all them chinky eye bitches look the same to me.* "Just hook me up, no flat chested, flat ass bitches Sora. I want the works. I'll start off wit' the hot shower massage."

"Follow me," she instructed Sandino with a devilish grin.

After entering through the wooden doors, the place was still a top of the line spot. He looked around in the spacious windowless lounge with mirrors on every wall and custom red couches with about ten girls sitting in sexy nighties. It also had a huge bar, custom designed lighting with rice paper lanterns and high-end bamboo flooring. It definitely wasn't your average, back alley massage parlor.

Sora signaled to a girl with long black hair and a short white negligee to follow them as she led the way to a glass elevator and hit the 2nd floor. Sandino was impressed with her choice. She was a beautiful girl who appeared to mixed with black and Vietnamese with dark skin and high cheek bones. She even had a nice round ass and big breast, which was always a plus.

"Nice, very nice," Sandino said.

"This is Ming. Don't beat up my girl, okay? I'm warning you," Sora replied.

"Warnin' me...please. Y'all dirty bitches been abused all your life...Don't try to come to America and act like shit is different."

Sora knew better than to have a comeback. With Sandino being a VIP customer all she could do was roll her eyes.

Once inside the elevator, Ming leaned up against Sandino and rubbed on his chest. Sandino tapped his pocket to make sure he had condoms. When she tried to reach up and kiss him, he pushed her away.

"Hold up, bitch I don't know you like that yet," he told her.

"Oh, but you will," Sora addressed.

When the elevator door opened, Sora pointed to a private room over to the left. "Have fun, I will join you in a little while, be nice Sandino," Sora said before the elevator doors closed.

She knew Sandino could get a little rough with the girls at times. Even though she liked it, most of the other girls didn't.

As soon as the two of them entered the room, Ming didn't hesitate walking over to the elegant walk-in shower with limestone tile and turned on the water. Sandino sat down on the side of the bed and started undressing. Before he could finish unbuttoning his custom made dress shirt with monogrammed cuffs, Ming immediately took over the job.

"I make you feel real good daddy," she said.

Seconds later they walked to the shower and Sandino stood under the hot steamy water while she lathered his body. She then got down on her knees and washed between his legs with a loofa.

"I make you cum daddy," she advised.

Ming moved her hands forcefully onto his dick then to his balls. The lather from the exfoliating Dove bodywash gently glided her hands back and forth. Her soft, smooth, little fingers rubbed and maneuvered around his ass sending sensations across his entire body. The circular motion she used while massaging his dick was considered *The Hand Job Special*, after a few seconds Sandino felt himself about to cum.

"Damn, girl," was all he could mumble as he released on the shower floor.

She licked the cum from his dick and slid her tongue across the tip of the head before sliding it in her mouth, giving him *The Blowjob Special*. It was an experience like no other and Sandino could feel his knees getting weak as she continued to bob and slurp. No one could give head jobs like his Asian bitches. Moments later, he could feel his body jerking again as he pulled out and shot cum all over her face.

"Damn, baby!" he yelled out as he collapsed against the shower wall.

Never missing a beat, she continued massaging his body until Sandino caught a second wind. "Bring your ass to the bed," he said, stepping out of the shower.

He sat down on the bed, reached over in his pocket and grabbed a condom, then asked himself, where Sora was by now. When Ming got out the shower and dried off, she reached in the small dresser draw and sprayed on some perfume.

The minute Sandino smelled the aroma of *Creed*, which was Skye's favorite, he flipped out. With visions of his wife in his head he picked up the small framed girl and roughly threw her on the bed. He then slapped her several times across her face before covering her mouth so she couldn't scream. She was terrified and continuously shook her head no, but Sandino could care less.

With his other hand he placed the condom over his nine inch tool, closed his eyes, and fucked her full speed, pushing her legs back like a pretzel. He pumped even harder as the girl mumbled in pain.

A few minutes later the door flew open and Sora along with the gun toting security guy stood there were stern looks.

"Get off her and get out!" Sora shouted. "We not serve you anymore. What has happen to you Sandino? Ever since you been popping pills you been nuts. Please leave before I have to shoot you dead!"

Sandino let go of the girl and moved off the bed.

"You gone shoot me Sora? I thought we were better than that!"

"Put your clothes on and get out. I told you not to hurt my girls!" Sora said walking out the room with Ming who was scared shitless.

After Sora left, Sandino went into a total rage. He started tossing shit around in the room and yelling at the security guard who was standing at the door was with his arms folded and shaking his head.

"What the fuck your big ass shaking your head for? If you didn't have that gun I would fuck your ass up!"

The security guard ignored Sandino.

"You wish you could be me instead of working security in a massage parlor. Don't you big man?" Sandino taunted.

When the guard got tired of hearing Sandino's mouth, he took the clip out of his gun, laid it on the floor and walked toward him.

"You been talking shit ever since you walked in that door, and I'm tired of your fucking mouth. Just because you played football you think you can treat people any kind of way. Since you want to beat on women, I'ma beat on your ass," the security guard said.

He stood toe to toe with Sandino like they were at a prized fight.

"Come on muthafucka. We can do this shit." Sandino raised his fist and got into his boxer stance.

42

However, before Sandino could say another word, the guard punched him in the face so hard he was knocked out cold.

"Punk-ass," the guard said as he placed Sandino's clothes on his chest then dragged him to the front door. After dragging him outside butt ass naked, the security guard looked at Sandino one last time. "Maybe next time you'll learn how to show some respect!"

Chapter Six 🏈

    After driving for hours and crossing over into Georgia, Skye decided against going to see the waitress's sister. She also decided to head toward Atlanta instead of traveling north toward Savannah. She'd always enjoyed the city when Sandino played against the Falcons, so laying low in that area seemed to be a good idea. They eventually checked into a shabby-ass Super 8 Hotel, on Fulton Industrial Circle, about ten minutes from downtown Atlanta. At the time, Skye had no idea that it was a bad area until she not only realized that a strip club was located on the same block, but all the people hanging around outside looked like they were on drugs. She remembered thinking to herself after pulling into the parking lot that they should find somewhere else to stay, but she was dead tired. Not to mention, Super 8 seemed to be all she could afford.

    She'd been calling Asia from Kareem's phone non-stop after leaving Jacksonville, but she wasn't answering. At first Skye thought maybe it was because Asia didn't recognize the number, but after texting and letting Asia know she'd lost her phone, her friend still hadn't responded. With only a hundred dollars left to her name, Skye was beyond worried, especially since they only had enough money for one more night in the hotel, and she couldn't use her credit or check cards for fear of Sandino finding them. Something wasn't right and Skye prayed that Sandino hadn't gotten to Asia before she got her cash.

Jackie D.

We've gone over the plan a thousand fucking times and now this bitch doesn't wanna call back, Skye thought. *Now, we gotta stay in this dump.* Skye thought then looked around. *The T.V. only gets six channels, the shower drain was clogged, and the doors aren't secure.*

"We're at least supposed to be up in a Hyatt or Westin," Skye mentioned to herself.

After laying down for a few hours, Skye decided to get up and walk around outside to gather her thoughts since all the kids were asleep. As rowdy as they'd been since she checked in, Skye hoped they stayed asleep for the rest of the night. She needed time to herself. She had to get a game plan together although she had no idea what step to take first. Pacing back and forth with her mind focused on her children's well-being, Skye suddenly bumped into a tall, slender girl with a hideous pink wig on. As soon as the girl looked up to say, 'excuse me', she immediately noticed the concerned look on Skye's face.

"Are you okay?" the fake Nikki Minaj girl asked.

"Yes, I'm fine." Skye quickly turned her head.

"You don't look fine," the woman replied. "What are you doing out here all alone? If I were you, I would go back inside. This isn't the best neighborhood for a woman to be walking alone."

Skye appeared even more concerned, but didn't respond.

The woman extended her hand. "Hi. My name is Ivy. I'm in the room next to you. I saw you and your kids when you came in. If you don't mind me asking, what's a pretty woman like you doing in a place like this?"

"I'm just passing through," Skye said, wondering why she was all up in her business.

"You look like you running from something to me."

Skye looked at her wondering how she could tell that she was on the run.

"Like I said, I'm just passing through," Skye reiterated

"Well, if you need anything just holla. I'm usually around all day, but I leave by ten o'clock to go to work. I strip at the club called, Babes down the street," Ivy pointed.

Well, that explains that crazy-ass wig, Skye thought. "You don't look like a stripper," Skye said, eyeing the girl's slim frame. She didn't have tits or an ass.

"Yeah, never in my wildest dreams did I think I would ever be doing this, but I do what I have to do to put myself through school. I'm a senior at Spellman, and tuition ain't cheap. Not to mention, I have a daughter to take care of. My little girl is all I have, so I don't regret shaking my ass for cash to make sure we survive. A mother will do whatever she has to for her child."

"That's so true," Skye agreed.

Ivy eyed Skye's well-defined figure. "You're a pretty thing; you could make a lot of money down there working at the club with me.

Skye shot Ivy a crazed looked. "Oh, no. I don't think so."

"Well, if you're ever interested I could always hook you up. Two of our girls left last week anyway, so we need some fresh meat. You could make enough in one night to get yourself and your kids away from this place. You don't belong here baby."

"No thanks, I could never dance in front of a bunch of strange men," Skye replied.

"Okay, but let me know if you change your mind!" Ivy shouted as Skye turned around and walked away.

After getting back to the room, Skye continued to pace around as thoughts of her now hundred dollar life savings entered her mind. There was no way four people were going to survive with that little bit of money. Getting angry all over again, Skye wanted to call Asia once again, but decided against it.

"If her ass wanted to call, she would've called by now,"

Skye mumbled.

Grabbing her purse, she peered inside at the five twenty dollar bills again as if more money would suddenly appear. She then took deep breath thinking, *how hard could it be to strip? I took pole dancing classes before, and used to give Sandino strip tease shows all the time before he lost his damn mind.*

After staring at the money for several more minutes, Skye walked over and woke Kareem up. "Hey," she said, shaking his shoulder. Kareem slowly opened his eyes. "Listen, I need to run out for a little while."

"Where are you going?" He questioned in a groggy tone.

"I'm just running out to the store. Please make sure the door is locked when I leave, and I don't care what the circumstances are. If anyone knocks on this door, don't answer it. You know to call 911, if anything gets out of hand, right?"

Kareem shook his head. "Of course."

"Okay…I'll be back in a little while. Try not to sleep too hard just in case Payton starts crying."

After giving her son a quick kiss on his forehead, Skye walked out the room and then knocked on Ivy's door.

"What time are we leaving?" she asked.

🏈🏈🏈🏈🏈🏈🏈

Three hours later, Skye stood outside the owner of the strip club's office door. She was so nervous her palms wouldn't seem to stop sweating. Skye hoped he didn't think she was some type of prostitute chick or had planned to do this long term. She was only there to make some fast cash and keep it moving…nothing more. She also hoped that she'd put on enough Mac foundation around her eye area, so the guy wouldn't think she was in trouble.

Skye fixed the awful, auburn-colored shoulder-length wig that she'd ran out and got from a beauty supply store before leaving the hotel with Ivy. She even bought some fake brown colored contacts to cover her piercing green eyes.

Realizing she wasn't dressed that sexy, Skye tried to brush the wrinkles out of her t-shirt with her hands, but it was no use; it definitely looked as if she'd slept in it. She then pushed her perky breasts up high so they were at least budging out from the top. Lastly, Skye reached in her purse, grabbed a mint and popped in her mouth hoping to hide the smell of Hennessey on her breath. She'd stopped by the bar on her way to the office and got a drink to try and calm her nerves, but it wasn't working.

"Get yourself together," she said before knocking on the door.

"Come in!" a man yelled.

When Skye walked inside, the owner was standing at the window with his back toward the door staring out the window as if he were deep in thought. He was a large man with a gleaming bald head and handsome features reminding her of Suge Knight. He even wore a red graphic print t-shirt with old-school red and white Air Force One's.

Skye cleared her throat. "Hello, I was told by Ivy I could come see you about a job."

He turned around looking Skye up and down with a smile on his face. "Yeah she told me, but damn Shawty...you fine as hell. Turn around and let me see what you working with."

Skye was totally caught off guard, but turned around in a circle.

"Oh you got both the b's, beauty and body, but can your ass dance is the question?" When he reached over and cut on some music, *Pop That Coochie* by 2 Live Crew blasted in his office. "Get your ass over there and let me see what you can do."

It's for your kids...it's for your kids, Skye thought as she hesitantly walked over to the stripper pole in the corner of his office.

She cringed at the thought of what nasty bitch had just touched the eight foot pole, but managed to block it out of her mind. She hoped all the pole dancing classes she took and the tricks she'd learned such as the butterfly and the twister would help her get the job.

As soon as Skye hit the pole and did her thing; the owner sat on the edge of his chair with excitement the entire time. About ten minutes into her routine, he turned the music off.

"You're hired pretty lady. You can go on at midnight. Damn, you dance sexy as shit. What's your name anyway?"

Suddenly the nick name Skye's father used to call her when she was a little girl popped in her head. "Precious!"

❦❦❦❦❦❦❦❦

At exactly 11:35 p.m., Skye sat on the edge of the bench in the dressing room oiling up her body thinking, *why do men love this greasy shit?*

She quickly slid on a pair of high-cut red lace thongs along with a matching bra and some platform heels that she'd borrowed from Ivy. Along with the shoes being a size too small, Skye prayed she didn't catch a disease from wearing the panties. Ivy didn't seemed like a trifling person, but you could never underestimate anyone's cleanliness.

She sprayed some Victoria's Secret shimmering body mist that she found in a locker all over her then turned and looked in the mirror. She was glad that Ivy had applied even more makeup to cover her bruises.

As Skye continued to stare into the mirror, tears rolled down her face as thoughts about what she was about to do danced around her head. She'd gone from a lifestyle of popping designer tags on a regular basis and never having to worry about money to stripping to keep a roof over their head and food in their mouths. It hurt knowing what result she'd come to, but what other choice did she have?

After taking a large sip from a Hennessey bottle inside Ivy's locker, she headed to the stage. As she peeped her head out and watched Ivy shaking her small ass to the thick crowd, Skye's nervousness went into overdrive.

"You can do this Skye, you can do this Skye," she chanted to herself.

As soon as Ivy's song ended and a new one came on, Skye heard the DJ saying, "We got a new booty in the house tonight y'all, so make her feel welcome. Please welcome to the stage, Miss Precious."

That was her cue.

Skye closed her eyes then took a deep breath before running out on stage to all the loud handclaps. She did every move and trick she could think of, while scooping up piles of money at the same time. Skye smiled thinking, *this should last us a few more nights*.

Jackie D.

Chapter Seven 🏈

The sound of Kareem and Jordan yelling woke Skye up the next morning. She hadn't had much sleep with all the loud noises and heavy traffic coming from the Interstate, so she felt exhausted. She reached over in the bed that felt like she was sleeping on concrete and felt for Payton. Realizing that she was laying right beside her, sound asleep, Skye kissed her forehead and placed a pillow on both sides to make sure she didn't fall off the bed.

Once she heard the sound of broken glass and the boys scuffling, she quickly jumped off of the bed, wondering what the hell was going on. "What are you doing Kareem? Get off your brother, you know better than to hit him," Skye said pulling the two boys apart.

The rage in Kareem's face instantly reminded her of Sandino. However, Jordan obviously wasn't going out like a punk because as soon as Skye released her grip, he dove right for his brother. They started fighting again.

"Stop that shit right now!" Skye yelled at the top of her lungs. She pulled Jordan away and slung him on the other side of the room then grabbed Kareem by his shirt.

All the yelling instantly woke up Payton, who was now screaming.

"Sit down…both of you. I can't even get a minutes rest without y'all acting like thugs on the damn street," Skye said, before grabbing the baby. The boys were still sitting with their arms crossed ready for war as she eyed them both. "Okay, who's going to tell me what all this fighting is about?"

"Kareem was on the phone. When I asked him who he was talking to, he got mad and started hitting me. He always trying to push me around and when I don't listen he will start punching on me and I'm tired of it," Jordan stated.

Skye looked over at Kareem. "Who were you talking to Kareem? And how long has this been going on? You two are supposed to take care of each other. I don't like the way you've been acting lately."

"I wasn't even on the phone. Jordan always running his mouth, so I had to take care of the situation like dad. He doesn't listen so he got hit," Kareem blurted out with a slight smirk.

Skye passed the baby to Jordan and walked over to her oldest son. "So, you think getting hit is funny?" When Kareem turned his head, her voice escalated. "Do you?"

"No," he answered.

"I didn't think so. Your father abusing me wasn't right, that's why I left him. I just want what's best for you guys. You might not realize that now, but you will later."

"I doubt it, your monkey-ass don't even know where we're going to live. This place is awful. I can't believe you got us up in here," Kareem mumbled.

When Skye heard her son call her the cruel name Sandino used sometimes, she walked over and grabbed him by the collar then pushed his body against the wall. "Son, don't get it twisted. I don't like to fight, but I will fuck your ass up right now if you ever disrespect me like that again!" Kareem just stared at his mother. It was a side of her that he'd never seen before. "Do you understand?"

"Yes," Kareem said, lowering his head.

After letting him go, Skye took a deep breath to try and get herself together. Kareem was definitely pushing it and she didn't know how much longer she could hold it together.

"I wanna go home. Can't you and dad get some type of

therapy or something?" Kareem asked. "He was supposed to take me to get my license. Now how am I supposed to get my car?"

When Skye felt herself getting ready to lose it again, she ran into the bathroom and slammed the door. Almost instantly she started hyperventilating and broke down into a silent sob.

"How am I going to raise three kids on my own? I know single mothers do it every day, but I don't think I'm strong enough to do this." Skye put her head in her lap as she sat on the bathroom floor crying her eyes out. She was an emotional wreck. She sat in a daze for what seemed like forever until she heard a slight tap at the door.

"Come in," Skye said.

Jordan peeked his head inside the door. "Ma, are you alright? You been in here a long time." A few seconds later, he made his way inside and sat down beside her.

"Is the baby okay?" Skye asked with concern.

"Yeah. I fed her a bottle and burped her then she went back to sleep. I took care of things," Jordan stated proudly.

Along with his height, Skye realized just how much her son was growing up. Moments later, Skye looked up and saw Kareem peeking his head in the door, too.

"You can come in," she stated.

He came in and stood against the wall looking sad and confused. Skye was concerned about Kareem. After watching his behavior and the look in his eyes earlier, she knew he would probably need some type of therapy. He had a violent streak just like Sandino, and that's the last thing she wanted.

"Sorry for calling you out your name, Ma," Kareem said.

"I'll accept your apology, but don't let it happen again," Skye advised.

"It won't," Kareem quickly replied.

"Are you all hungry?" she asked. Both Jordan and Kareem shook their heads at the same time. "Well, let's go get something to eat. I saw a McDonald's down the street. I think getting out will do us all some good. We haven't even been in this room long and it's already driving us crazy."

"Ma, I don't want McDonalds. Can we go to Joe's Stone Crab? Do they have one here?"

Skye couldn't help but laugh. Her kids were definitely spoiled when it came to food most of the time. "No son. I'm afraid we're gonna have to hit up the dollar menu until I talk to Asia. Gotta spend our money wisely." She planned to make the stripper money last.

Before leaving, Skye put on the wig that she used at the strip club along with the fake contacts. She didn't want anybody to necessarily recognize, Precious, but she also didn't want anybody to see her real features either.

"Why are you even wearing that thing?" Kareem questioned.

"Because it makes me feel a little more comfortable with it on. I'm hoping we won't get recognized like this," Skye advised.

"But we don't have on disguises," Jordan butted in.

"I know, but I'm planning on buying you and Kareem wigs today."

Jordan put his hands in the air. "Oh noooooo. Nope, I'm not wearing no wig."

Skye chuckled then pulled out a twenty dollar bill and left the rest of the money so she wouldn't be tempted to spend it. Skye scanned the room making sure all the bags were packed and ready just in case they had to leave in a hurry. After changing Payton's diaper they headed out the door and down the stairs.

They hadn't even made it to the car before Skye caught a glimpse of a weird looking black dude going up the stairs that gave her an eerie feeling. Even though he was yet another crazy looking junkie, she brushed it off as being paranoid and headed toward the car.

Thirty minutes later, she and the boys were all enjoying a hot batch of fries when Skye noticed a man in a nice suit watching them closely. A few minutes later the man approached them, which instantly made Kareem stop eating. He eyeballed the stranger closely.

"Hello. I hate to bother you all, but my name is Deacon Jones," he greeted. "You look like you need help my sister, I have connections to a woman's battered shelter if you need it," he said handing Skye a card. It was at that time when she noticed a thick Bible in his hand.

"Oh, thank you, but I'll be okay," Skye replied in an embarrassed tone. She realized she'd left her sunglasses in the room, exposing her black eye for all to see.

The Deacon stood shaking his head. "I don't understand why any man would do that to such a pretty face, please make that call if you ever change your mind."

Just before leaving the table, he winked at Skye then turned around. *A Deacon winking… What the hell is up with this neighborhood,* she thought. *I really need to get in touch with Asia.*

As soon as the Deacon walked away, Kareem started breathing heavy and complaining. "Why can't we just go back home? I'm not going to any shelter. What kind of mother would take her kids to a shelter? Dad promised he wouldn't hit you anymore if we came back home."

Skye's eyes increased as she looked over at Kareem. "Have you talked to your father? Did you tell him where we were?"

"Yeah, I talked to him, but I didn't tell him where we were," Kareem lied. "He said he was sorry and had a big surprise for you."

Realizing that Sandino was probably half-way to Georgia by now, Skye jumped up, and told the boys to come on. Despite them telling her that they weren't finished eating, Skye quickly made her way to the car and jumped inside. Making a mental note to call Asia again, she was prepared to leave Atlanta and drive somewhere else to keep from being found.

Skye yelled at Kareem all the way back to the hotel so he had a clear understanding that he'd put all their lives in jeopardy. She even demanded that he hand over his phone and instantly threw it out the window. Realizing that he'd made a major mistake, Kareem remained mute and showed no expression until his mother opened the door to their room. They all stood in total shock at the damage.

You would've thought Hurricane Katrina had just touched down the way the room had been ransacked. It also didn't take much to realize that they'd been robbed. All their possessions that were worth something were gone. Kareem's G-Shock watch, Jordan's DS game system, her diamond earrings along with the six hundred dollars Skye earned stripping that she'd hid inside the nightstand was now gone. Although their clothes had been pulled out of the suitcases and thrown all over the room, luckily they were still there.

"I can't believe this!" Kareem yelled.

"Come on, let's go," Skye said.

"Ma, aren't we gonna call the police?" Jordan questioned.

Even though it wasn't Sandino's style, Skye knew it was a possibility that he was behind this. She then thought about the suspicious looking man walking up the steps as they left. As questions bounced around her head, she had no idea who was responsible for the robbery, but didn't plan to stick around and find out.

"No, let's go!" she demanded.

They quickly grabbed their things throwing what they could back into the suitcases and ran down the stairs. Suddenly, Ivy came out of her room, and ran to the railing. "Precious, where are you going? What's wrong?" she yelled.

Not knowing if Ivy had anything to do with the robbery,

Skye ignored her before they jumped into the Honda and skidded out the parking lot. With her adrenaline at another all time high, Skye looked in her rear view mirror to see if anyone was following them. That's when she noticed a gold Tahoe with tinted windows hot on her trail. Her heart raced as she turned the corner going well over the speed limit. Skye clutched the wheel tightly never taking an eye off the Tahoe while switching lanes and swerving in and out of traffic.

"See what you did Kareem? Dad is trying to kill all of us, he'll never change. When will you ever get that into your messed up brain?" Jordan yelled.

When Kareem reached over and punched Jordan on his arm, Skye felt like she was about to lose her mind. Now wasn't the time to be bickering with each other, and apparently her speech from earlier hadn't worked.

Just as Skye was about to flip out, she spotted a parked police car on the side of the street. Trying desperately to get his attention, she quickly increased her speed, did an unsafe lane change then blew her horn non-stop. Within seconds, the police officer had his blue lights on and quickly headed in her direction. Strangely, when Skye looked back, the gold Tahoe was nowhere to be found.

Chapter Eight 🏈

Skye pulled the car over on the side of the dark road and watched as the officer approached her car. As soon as he tapped on the window with his flash light, she rolled it down.

"License and registration please, are you aware how fast you were driving? You could've killed someone dipping in and out of lanes like that. Have you been drinking?" he questioned.

Skye looked in her purse for her license without saying a word as tears began to pour down her face.

The officer shined his flash light in the car and noticed her crying and the bad bruises on her face. When Payton started to whine, he shined the light toward the back and saw the frightened looks on the boys' faces. "Are you in some type of trouble Miss.?"

Skye broke down instantly. "My husband is trying to kill us. He was driving a gold Tahoe. That's why I was driving like that. I was trying to escape."

"Your husband was chasing you?" the officer asked trying to understand her story.

"I'm not sure it was him, I didn't see the driver's face, but my husband is crazy. He could've hired someone. Please help me," she pleaded.

The officer gave Skye a skeptical look like she was making the entire story up, but the bruises and the sad looks on all their faces quickly convinced him that something had to be wrong. He put out a description of the vehicle. "Is there some place I can escort you?"

With no place to go and no money, Skye gave him the card from the deacon. The office took the card and went back to his car. After placing the call, the deacon provided the officer with the information to the secret shelter and he agreed to take them. Skye reassured her sons, it was only temporary.

🏈🏈🏈🏈🏈🏈🏈🏈

Justice looked at his watch; he was almost finished with his last exit interview for the evening. Several of the women and their families were leaving the shelter and moving into places of their own, which always required a lot of paperwork.

Justice enjoyed helping the families, but he was growing tired of the same old routine associated with the shelter. He never knew how difficult it would be dealing with a bunch of hormonal women day after day. This wasn't the big plan he visualized for Breaking the Cycle women's shelter. A safe haven he'd opened in memory of his mother who was abused and killed by his father who later turned the gun on himself when Justice was only eight years old.

He directed his attention to Deidra, who'd completed her last piece of paper work for her new apartment. Deidra and her son had come to the shelter six months ago after a terrifying experience.

"Okay Deidra, you've completed all your paperwork, so we're done here. It's certainly been a pleasure having you here. You were always strong enough to stand on your own. We just gave you the reassurance you needed." Justice stood up and gave her a hug.

"Thanks for everything Justice, I don't know what I would've done if you and BTC hadn't helped my son and I."

Deidra squeezed Justice so tight, she almost took his breath away. She was a big girl, about 300lbs. Justice often wondered how any man could beat her ass.

Once she released her grip, Justice fixed his shirt. "The movers will be here in a few hours to help you move all your belongings. Make sure you sign my boy, Malik, up for a little league baseball team, he got skills. You did a wonderful job raising him. Pat yourself on the back mama."

Deidra wiped a tear from her eye. "Thanks again Justice. You've always been such a sweetheart," she said leaving the office.

Justice sat back down and shuffled through the huge stack of papers on his mahogany desk. He dropped his head thinking about how long it was going to take him to finish up. A sudden knock on his office door startled him.

"Come in!" he yelled.

When his assistant, Mercedes, pranced inside she was popping gum as usual wearing her usual cheap platform heels. She was your typical Puerto Rican girl with thick, full lips that always displayed gold lipstick and dark lip liner. Her long jet black hair had golden highlights, which she always wore in an outdated, crimped hair style.

"Excuse me Justice, Deacon Jones is on line one for you. Do you need me to help out with any of that paperwork?" She walked over to his desk and quickly sat on the edge. "I'm sure you remember what happened the last time we worked late."

Mercedes leaned over revealing her 36D cup sized breasts. It was the one asset she was truly proud of. "Don't you remember having these babies in your mouth? Remember how many times you kept telling me how perfect my nipples were."

"Knock it off Mercedes. I told you before, us sleeping together was a mistake," Justice said.

"You could've fooled me. The way you were moaning didn't sound like a mistake baby."

She rubbed her hands against his low cut hair then down his face.

Justice immediately pushed her hand away. "Mercedes, I told you I don't want to jeopardize our working relationship. Besides I'm not feeling you like that. You need to forget that shit ever happened. Get out of my face anyway. You smell like cigarettes."

"You weren't complaining about the smell when you were in between my pussy," Mercedes shot back. "I can't forget about that night, and neither can you, no matter how hard you try to front like it didn't mean anything. I know it meant something."

"It didn't."

"Stop lying," Mercedes replied before jumping off the desk, sashaying out the office and closing the door.

Realizing that he needed to find another assistant, Justice shook his head before picking up the receiver and pushing line one. "Hello, Deacon Jones."

"Hey Justice, how are you?

"Busy as usual. What can I do for you?"

"I met a young lady and her kids today, she was badly beaten. I gave her a card and didn't really think she would contact me, but I received a call from an officer saying she was running from her husband. He's escorting them there. They should arrive within minutes. She has a very pleasant sprit, I watched her interact with her three kids and she seems to be a loving mother. She's a beautiful woman as well."

Justice chuckled. "I know where you're going with this. I don't mix business with pleasure Deacon."

"Yes, I know, but I have a feeling you might make an exception on this one," the Deacon said.

"Are you sure you weren't interested in her?" Justice joked.

"No, son…not at all."

"Whatever you say. So, I guess you're trying to set me up."

"I promised your mother I would look after you boys

and I'm a man of my word Justice."

"Okay Deacon, I'll be expecting them. We have three families moving out this week so it's plenty of room. I'll talk to you later," Justice replied then hung up.

Moments later, he started the paperwork for the new arrival, which was the part he hated the most. He didn't like to see the women when they first arrived. They were so mentally and physically hurt, most times he could hardly take it.

When opening the shelter he planned to be more of a behind the scenes owner. He had hopes that Mercedes would be the perfect candidate to run the business, but after monitoring her behavior and how she sometimes looked down on some of the women, he realized that her heart wasn't genuine. How quickly she'd forgotten that she too was just like them when she first came to the shelter.

Plus she was more interested in fucking him instead of handling things on a professional level. She'd let her emotions get in the way. Justice had to admit, Mercedes was fine, but he really regretted sleeping with her. Ever since that night, she'd been acting crazy as hell. To make matters worse, Justice couldn't stand her two bad ass sons.

He never meant to get involved with a woman he worked with or someone who was a former occupant. He was there to help the women...dating them wasn't an option. He didn't have the heart to build them up and when things didn't work out, break them down again. If Mercedes didn't get herself together Justice knew he'd have to let her go.

He listened as kids ran up and down the hall. After only a year and a half of running the shelter he wanted to do something different already. Justice had several profitable organizations interested in taking over, and after he tied up some loose ends he was going to think about stepping away.

Opening up a few envelopes with his letter opener, the big read letters reading PAST DUE on his utility bill made Justice shake his head.

Jackie D.

"These fucking bills never stop," he mumbled to himself. After opening up his mortgage bill that said the exact same thing, he threw the papers to the side.

Justice looked up at the clock and decided to buckle down and knock out the paperwork. Hopefully he could get out in time to see the Monday night football game. He grabbed his IPod and placed the small white earplugs in his ears. The lyrics from his favorite rapper, Jay-Z echoed in his ears.

"If you're having' girl problems I feel bad for you son, I got 99 problems, but a bitch ain't one!"

You got that right Jay, he thought.

Chapter Nine 🏈

Skye drove behind the police car closely as the officer escorted them to the shelter near Stone Mountain. Even though he was way out of his jurisdiction, he wanted to make sure Skye and the kids arrived safely. While driving, Skye kept looking in her rear view for signs of the Tahoe, but the truck never reappeared. She was definitely confused. Even though Skye didn't get a good look at the driver, and she knew Sandino wouldn't have trashed the room, she still didn't wanna ignore the fact that he could've been behind of all this.

Skye watched as they drove another ten minutes before turning down a dark, poorly lit road and drove a few more miles into a deep secluded area. *Nobody's gonna find this shit,* she thought. Minutes later they finally pulled up to a white colonial style house that sat on about an acre and a half of land. The house was in desperate need of a paint job, but the two big columns in front and rocking chairs added lots of charm.

Skye turned off the car and turned around. "Listen up guys, when we get in there, we can't tell anyone who your father is. It'll be safer that way. Don't even mention him."

"I still don't understand why we gotta come here," Kareem said looking around. "This place don't look right."

"Look, I'm not thrilled about this either, but right now we don't have much of a choice."

"How long are we gonna stay?" Jordan asked.

"Hopefully not long. As soon as I talk to Asia and she sends us some money, we can leave. Whoever broke into our room stole all we had left." Both of the boys were quiet. "I promise. Things will work out."

"Okay," Jordan said. Kareem replied shortly after.

"While we're staying here, I'm gonna be using the name Janelle," Skye informed them.

"Do you have to change ours? I like my name," Jordan said with a concerned expression.

"It probably would've been better if we changed your names too, but something tells me you're gonna forget anyway, so you all can continue to use your real ones. But don't tell anyone our last name is Washington. We'll use Coleman for now. Got it?" When both boys shook their heads, Skye adjusted her wig then opened the door. "Okay, let's go."

They all got out the car, grabbed their bags and walked behind the officer. He kept looking at Skye like he wanted to ask her more questions but didn't. Moments after ringing the doorbell, Mercedes came to the door.

"May I help you?" She held a stern look.

"Is Mr. Mitchell here? I'm officer Hicks. Deacon Jones should've called, he's expecting us."

"Who?" Mercedes looked as if she was expecting him to say something else.

The officer looked at her, then remembered the deacon saying, "if you don't know the password you won't be allowed inside."

Skye put her bags down and was getting ready to speak when the officer stopped her.

"Oh, yes…Breaking the Cycle," he blurted out.

"Thank you, welcome to BTC, come on in," Mercedes replied with a smile now formed on her face.

Once inside, Skye noticed the tall ceilings, beautiful woodwork and old antique maple floors. However, all that changed as soon as Mercedes escorted them inside a large family room that was really outdated with purple shag carpet and striped wall paper. Mercedes told Skye and the boys to have a seat on the old cracked leather couch.

Jordan looked around wondering how many families lived inside the large crowded house. It was shit everywhere.

"I'll be right back," Mercedes said then told the officer to follow her down the hall to see Mr. Mitchell.

Sticking out like a sore thumb, it didn't take long for everyone in the house to direct their attention toward them. From the teenagers in the family room watching T.V. to the group of women peeking out from the kitchen, everyone was trying to figure out who they were because unlike most families who came, Skye and her family still looked like a million bucks to them. It was almost as if everyone could smell money.

All of a sudden one of the women who appeared to be in her late thirties spoke up. "What happened to you? Did your husband catch you charging too much on your *Saks* card? Or are you mad because your husband bought the Maserarti instead of the Aston Martin?" she laughed crazily.

Skye gritted her teeth and shot a look back thinking, *Bitch, you don't know me*!
She then turned her head and noticed a big, amazon looking woman staring at her, too. Skye stared back. "I'm not in the mood or have the strength to fight any of these bitches, but I will," she said to herself.

Within minutes, Mercedes finally returned and introduced herself. "Hi, I'm Mercedes Guzman. I work closely with Justice, I mean Mr. Mitchell, to insure that all the families are safe and comfortable during their stay here. I was once a victim of domestic violence and Breaking the Cycle was a safe haven for my kids and I. After the center helped me, I felt so strongly about helping other women, Mr. Mitchell asked me to stay and help run the place."

"Nice to meet you, I'm Janelle and these are my children, Kareem, Jordan and Payton," Skye responded.

Mercedes smiled at Payton then looked at the boys. "Hello handsome young men, nice to meet you. I have two son's as well, the two knuckle heads over there sitting on the love seat, Joey and Manny. They'll help you guys if you need anything around here," Mercedes said, pointing in their direction.

Skye looked at the Spanish decent woman along with the tight leggings and cropped leather jacket that barley covered her ass. *Damn the workers around here obviously don't have a dress code*, she thought.

Suddenly, Mercedes' cell phone rang and she excused herself and walked down the hall. At that moment, Skye saw the big girl roll her eyes at Mercedes then walk to her room.

Wonder what that shit is all about, Skye wondered.

A few minutes later the officer came back and asked Skye to come with him.

"I'll be right back," she told the boys then got up carrying Payton in her arms.

When Skye walked into the door of the office, Justice's eyes grew the size of an eight ball. His facial expression gave it away that he was taken aback by her beauty. He stood quiet for a second. At the same time, Skye's eyes zoomed in on Justice as well. At 5'10, a deep chocolate skin tone, nice build and thick goatee, he instantly reminded her of Lem from *Soul Food*. His fresh Hugo Boss shirt and True Religion jeans, told her he wasn't a bad dresser either. It was impossible not to admire how fine he was.

After Justice informed the officer that he could finally leave, he walked over and introduced himself. "Hello, I would like to welcome you. I'm Justice Mitchell the founder of BTC. I run the shelter, teach the self defense classes, and I'm also one of the counselors.

"Thank you, my name is Janelle Coleman," Skye said.

"Nice to meet you Janelle, but can I ask you a quick question?"

"Sure."

"Is Janelle Coleman your real name?" Justice asked.

Skye was caught completely off guard.

"Don't worry, you can trust us. At BTC, we don't disclose personal information to anyone. I'm actually the only one who has access to all the family files in my office, so your information is strictly confidential. We just like to start on honest terms," Justice assured.

Even though Justice seemed sincere, Skye still wasn't comfortable. "Yes, it is."

"Okay, great. Wow, look at this beautiful baby."

Payton grinned. With a head full of Sandino's curly hair and Skye's green eyes, she could've easily been in a Gerber commercial.

"Has anybody ever told you that you look like that girl from Flava of Love?"

Skye smiled. "Yes, Delicious right? I get it all the time."

"Yeah, Delicious. I mean y'all aren't identical, but you do favor each other. Your hair is a little different, but there's definitely a resemblance," Justice said. "Is that a wig?"

Skye felt so embarrassed. "Ummm…yes."

"Well, you don't have to hide here. Trust me, you can be yourself."

"Thanks, but for now, I'll just keep it on."

"Your choice. Anyway, back to business. I understand you have a situation with your husband following you. Is that correct?"

"Yes, my kids and I need a safe place to stay until I can get in touch with my friend to send me more money." Skye looked around in his office at the Psychology degree hanging on the wall.

"We have plenty of room. You guys can stay as long as

you need to. We have several programs to help you, find a place to live and a job."

A job? I haven't worked in years, who does that? Skye thought.

While Skye spoke to Justice, Kareem and Jordan watched an old Martin Lawrence show re-run with the rest of the kids. Most of them were laughing, but Mercedes' two sons watched them instead of the TV. The oldest son Joey, who seemed to be the ring leader around the house, whispered something to his brother and they both got up and walked over to Kareem and Jordan seconds later.

"Damn, y'all some rich niggas, huh? Don't nobody come in here rocking new Jordans and fresh Rock & Republic jeans. Me and my brother are gonna love wearing your gear."

When Joey walked up close to Kareem, he reached over on the table and grabbed an ink pen and stuck it up to Joey's neck. "Look muthafucka, I don't wanna have to fuck you and your punk-ass brother up! So, I advise you to leave me any my brother the fuck alone," he said, pushing the pen deep in Joey's skin.

When Kareem heard Skye coming back down the hall moments later, he quickly released the grip and removed the pen. "Keep your mouth shut," he demanded.

Jordan smiled as Joey and his brother walked away like two punks. For once, he was glad his brother was so violent.

Once Skye and Justice appeared, Justice extended his hand to the boys. "How are you young men doing?" he asked.

They both stood quiet looking at him like he was crazy.

"They're doing okay," Skye interrupted.

"Well, from what I hear, you boys have had quite a journey. Let me show you to your rooms. The boys can stay in our teen's quarters and Janelle, you and the baby can stay right down the hall."

The boys looked at their mother confused.

"Listen, Mr. Mitchell, my family and I have to stay together. If not, then we'll leave," Skye advised.

"It's your choice to leave Ms. Coleman. I'm here to help you and your family. If you all want to cram in one room, that's on you, follow me." Justice led them down the hall and pointed to a room. "We're in the middle of renovations. Some of the bedrooms are completed, but unfortunately the room you will be staying in tonight isn't. We have several families moving out this week and you can move into one of the nicer rooms then."

"Thanks," Skye answered. She felt bad about the room comment knowing he was only trying to help.

"Bathrooms are down the hallway. Have a good night," Justice said before walking off.

Once Skye opened the door and they all walked inside, she locked it. After handing the baby to Kareem, she then pushed a small dresser up against the door. Although Justice seemed cool, Skye didn't trust him or any of the people staying in the house, so she didn't want to take any chances.

When she looked around the room, it had the same hideous 1970 purple shag carpet, and a stale smell that reminded her of moth balls and old bread. She wanted to cry, but what other choice did they have? It was either stay until she could reach Asia for more money or go running back to Sandino and pray that he wouldn't kill her ass.
She decided to stay; she was never going back to that life.

"Come on boys, let's try and get some sleep," she suggested.

As they all curled up together on the dingy lumpy mattress, Kareem hugged his mother for the first time since they left Florida.

"I'm sorry I called dad. I really thought since he might've missed us he would stop taking the pills and things would go back to the way they used to be, but I was wrong. I promise…I'll protect and take care of us from now on."

Chapter Ten

Sandino rolled over in bed with mixed emotions after receiving the call from Kareem. He sat up and thought about what his son had just said to him especially the part about getting help. Kareem seemed very upset and blamed his father for ruining their family, which surprisingly hurt Sandino a bit.

"Dad, you told me and Jordan the horrible stories about the way your father treated you growing up. You promised us you would be a better father, but you lied. You're no different than he was," Kareem kept saying.

Sandino wasn't surprised by Kareem's words. He knew his son was tough and had his same kick ass mentality. He also knew what he needed to say in order to get in his son's good graces, even if it was a lie.

He told Kareem he was going into rehab once they came back home. He went on to explain that the pills were the reason he'd been acting crazy and abusing his mother. Sandino then told Kareem that he really missed them and promised to never take another pill or hit his mother again.

When Sandino could tell Kareem was softening up, he asked him where they were. Minutes later, Sandino displayed a wide grin when his son told him they were in Atlanta. Unfortunately, the phone went dead before Sandino could get an address or exact location, but he was satisfied for now.

Sandino dialed Black's cell phone again, who was actually right downstairs. He'd tried to call Black a few times right after Kareem called, but Black never answered. With Sandino's knee acting up once again, calling Black would save him a trip from having to move at that moment. Ever since the injury, his knee was known to do that from time to time, which is another reason why Sandino stayed so angry a lot of times. When Black still didn't answer, this time Sandino limped out the room, and down the steps.

"Yo Black, I found her ass. She's in ATL some damn where. Get yo' shit. We're gonna catch a flight this time!" Sandino yelled. He'd been so tired and worn out from chasing Skye the day before there was no way he was about to do the same thing all over again.

When there was no response, Sandino opened the door to the guest room to find Black and some fat trick passed out naked on the bed with a plate of cocaine sitting between them.

"Black!" Sandino yelled. "Get your ass up. I tried to tell you this shit last night, but you were fucked up then, too." As soon as Black mumbled something and turned over, Sandino slammed the door.

"I can't deal wit' this bullshit my knee is killin' me."

It was obvious that Black wasn't reliable like Cruze, and at a time like this, Sandino needed his friend by his side. Unfortunately, after they got back to Miami, Cruze asked Sandino to drop him off in Overtown and hadn't been heard from since. Sandino wasn't the type to kiss anybody's ass, but regretted the way he treated him. Besides, Cruze was really the only true friend Sandino had. He pulled out his phone to call Cruze, but quickly changed his mind.

"Fuck that nigga, I don't need him, I'm Sandino Washington! Niggas sweat me, not the other way around."

He limped back to his room and grabbed his bottle of Oxycontin off the night stand then dropped five tablets into his pill crusher until they were completely powder. He poured the powder on a mirror, straightened out three long lines with a razor, grabbed a straw and started sniffing aggressively. He then walked into the bathroom, grabbed the small mirror that held the left over cocaine from the night before and snorted a line of that as well.

Moments later, Sandino laid back and prepared for his high to kick in. When thoughts of his family tapped danced around in his head, Sandino glided his hand over the spot where Skye slept. He really wished he could control his temper and stop beating on her so they could be a family, but the truth was…he couldn't.

$$\mathcal{SSSSSSS}$$

An hour and several cocaine lines later, Sandino abruptly jumped up off the bed and immediately started throwing shit around the room, especially frames that held pictures of Skye and the kids at several vacation spots.

"Skye, if you don't bring yo' ass home, please believe that you will never live a normal fuckin' life!" he shouted as if she could hear him.

Looking at a picture of Skye in Barbados before she had Payton, thoughts of another man touching her model-like figure popped into his head. She was gorgeous, and the thought of her possibly spending time with another man really enraged him. Suddenly, he fell to his knees with visions of his childhood in mind.

"It's Peaches' fault that I lost my fuckin' family. If she'd been a better mother I wouldn't have turned out like this!" Sandino belted. He then jumped up and started pacing the floor. "You know what… I'm goin' to see that bitch. Some-body gotta pay for this shit," he said throwing on some sweat pants.

He hadn't seen his mother in over four months. Even though they'd been on speaking terms for years, Sandino had yet to confront her about his feelings, so it was still hard for him to forgive her. The memories of how she'd let his father abuse them his entire childhood always seemed to settle into Sandino's thoughts, causing their rocky relationship to go months without communication. She'd never even met Payton. He promised himself he would never treat women the way his father did, but instead he ended up being just like him.

"The sorry muthafucka even had the nerve to die before I got a chance to tell 'em how much of a fucked up father he was," Sandino said.

Snorting the last line, Sandino grabbed his keys, ran out the house, then jumped in his car. Yelling from the time he backed out of his driveway all the way to Coconut Grove, Sandino was pretty fired up when he pulled up in front of his mother's house.

"Let me grab this, just in case," Sandino said about the .45 under his seat. "As far as I know, she might have a boyfriend now, who might have to be dealt wit'."

Getting out of the car, Sandino power walked up to the front door, then banged on it with the side of his fist. Seconds later, a woman came to the door that looked exactly like his mother.

"Sandino Lamont Washington, stop banging on this damn door like you the police!"

He looked at his aunt, Shelly who he hadn't seen in awhile. She was still pretty, but had aged and put on at least fifteen pounds.

"Don't just stand there, bring your crazy ass in and give your auntie a hug."

Sandino walked into the house without even speaking yet alone hugging her. "Peaches!" he yelled.

Sandino walked back though the house he'd bought his mother when she finally decided to leave the rough Baltimore streets. She'd actually been in Florida longer than he had. When he heard music coming from the backyard, he quickly walked outside to find several of his family members drinking, cooking out on the grill and lounging by the pool. They seemed to be having a good time.

"Baby, your mother isn't here. She's in the hospital. She's very sick," Shelly informed. "I thought you knew."

Sandino suddenly had a change of heart about the reason for his visit when he heard the news. He stood for a minute gathering his thoughts. "What's wrong with her? Why didn't anybody call me and tell me my mother was in the hospital? Y'all muthafuckas know how to call when you need some damn money!"

"Don't disrespect me," Shelly shot back. "I'm still your aunt."

"Why didn't someone call me?" Sandino repeated.

"My brother did call you…several times actually, but you never answer your damn phone. Hell, I even tried to call your house, but your crazy ass has the number changed every week."

"What about Skye?"

Shelly let out a slight laugh. "Tried that too…she never answers either. Y'all probably thought we were calling for some money."

Sandino's demeanor finally softened a bit. "So, what's wrong wit' her?"

"She has lung cancer," his aunt replied.

Rage instantly came upon him once again. He looked at his aunt and the rest of her family. The same family who would never help or give his mother a place to stay when they were running from his father.

"So, y'all sittin' around here havin' fun when my mother up in the hospital sick?" Sandino didn't even wait for a response before he pulled out his gun and fired several shots in the air. All the family members instantly started running. You would've thought Sandino was Nino Brown from the movie *New Jack City* from the fear everyone now seemed to have. His aunt tried to calm him down as the rest of the family members scattered.

Jackie D.

"All y'all free loaders got two hours to get the fuck out my mother's house or I'm comin' back and burn this mutha-fucka down. And I won't care who the hell is in it!"

Chapter Eleven

Asia drove down from the hair salon admiring how good she looked in the rear view mirror. Trying a new quick weave, she liked the way her stylist made the jet black layered bob look like her natural hair as she stopped at a red light. Quickly grabbing her new Pink 4 Friday M.A.C. lip gloss by Nicki Minaj, Asia applied a thick coat just before the light changed. Men seemed to love looking at her shiny, luscious lips, so weekly trips to the infamous cosmetic store was a must.

After throwing the gloss back into her purse she realized she had two missed calls. Not recognizing the number, Asia pulled off then decided to check her voicemail before calling the number back. Entering her pass code, she placed her Blackberry on speaker then listened as Sandino yelled to the top of his lungs.

"Oh, I see you haven't been back to work in three days, huh? You haven't even been home. What…are you scared, bitch? Well you should be because I checked my account and I see that Skye withdrew over $70,000 of my fuckin' money. I know you helped her because her dumb-ass couldn't have done it without you. What…were you on some 'ole get back shit because I didn't want your dried up pussy anymore after we fucked? You better hope I don't find your ass because when…"

Cutting the message off, Asia hit the number nine to save it just in case she needed it for proof that he was harassing her. She sighed as she listened to another message from Sandino.

"Bitch, I'm tellin' you. Just like you helped her steal my shit, I suggest you help her put it back into my damn account A.S.A.P. I'm warnin' you Asia!"

Hitting the number nine again Asia saved that message just like all the others. Ever since Sandino showed up at the bank, he'd been calling and threatening her non-stop. Afraid of what he might do, Asia decided to take some time off work then called Keon and asked if she could stay with him for a while. Not only did she need his dick since they'd been sexing every night, she also needed him for protection. She'd even purchased a gun and carried it around just in case his huge build wasn't enough. If Keon couldn't defend her, one of the twelve rounds would.

When Asia's mind suddenly drifted to Skye, she felt really bad for ignoring all her calls. Skye had been a good friend to her, so it bothered Asia that she not only fucked her husband but that she never had any intentions on sending Skye the money. Her bank account was empty from all the shopping, her penthouse apartment, and the truck that she couldn't afford.

Feeling guilty, she picked up her phone and thought about calling Kareem's number back to at least tell Skye how sorry she was, but she quickly changed her mind. Instead, she hit *2 on the keypad and followed the instructions to get to a Sprint representative.

"Hello, my name is Asia Jones and I would like to have my phone number changed effective immediately," she said once an operator finally answered.

After ending the call, Asia thought about how she could hardly wait to see Keon. Her juicy pussy was a magnet to men. Once men got a taste, they were hooked and she had plans for his ass. She was going against her rule of being with a man too long, but his good dick was worth bending the rules this once.

Twenty minutes later, Asia pulled up in front of Keon's Bay View Plaza condo in Miami Beach. She loved his place and loved staying there. Once she parked in the underground parking lot, Asia got out and walked to the door leading to the elevators and punched in Keon's code. When she got off the elevator on the eighteenth floor, Asia used the key Keon had given her, turned the knob and walked inside.

The smell of something cooking immediately entered her nostrils.

"Keon!" she called out. Asia walked past the dining room, where there were lit candles on a table and an elegant setting for two. "Wow," she said, inhaling the aroma of a vanilla scent.

Moments later, she noticed a note on the coffee table that said, *Open M*e. Asia looked around smiling like a school girl.

***Welcome home beautiful. The meal is almost ready, follow the rose petals I have a surprise for you upstairs* .**

Asia smiled thinking, *home*, but continued following the petals up the small spiral staircase. When she reached the top step, she saw another note.

Drop those clothes and continue following the petals into the bedroom.

Smiling again, Asia took off her clothes then followed the petals into the bedroom and over to the king sized bed where another note sat.

***Open the blue box. Put what's inside on then follow the petals* .**

Asia saw another box with ribbons on the bed and wanted to open that one as well, but did as she was told. Opening the box, she was surprised to see a gorgeous red silk robe from Agent Provocateur.

Great taste, Asia thought to herself after slipping it on.

Once that was done, she followed the petals into the bathroom to find Keon standing beside his large Jacuzzi tub, naked and oiled up with his dick standing up at full attention. Asia dropped her new robe and grabbed Keon's extended hand as he escorted her into the hot soothing bubble bath. After pouring two glasses of champagne, he joined her. The sounds of Kem played from an I-pod as he pulled her toward his lips.

She looked at him, he looked at her. Within seconds, they were inside the Jacuzzi having hot passionate sex. The two connected as one as the water cascaded around their bodies. Asia rode and grinded him hard when she felt his massive dick vibrating inside her nest.

"Shit, this some good pussy," Keon said as his breathing increased.

Licking her nipples in a circular motion, he began to tug on them before fighting back the urge to cum. However, nothing worked. Within seconds, Keon's body started to jerk as he released. Asia squeezed her walls around his dick and bit down on her bottom lip as she moaned then exploded on her own. It was powerful.

Asia looked over at Keon thinking, d*amn, I've never had an orgasm like that.*

Once they both got out of the tub and dried off, they laid on the bed before Keon asked, "So when are you planning to tell me what happened? You've been over here for days." Asia looked hesitant. "You can trust me," he assured, rubbing her back.

Finally opening up, Asia told Keon everything that happened with Skye including the issue with Sandino and the money.

"Is Skye alright? Do you know where she is?" he questioned.

"No," Asia replied.

Keon looked at the way Asia continued to fidget as if she was telling a lie.

"Are you sure?" he asked.

"Yes, I haven't heard from her."

"What about the money? Did y'all take it?"

Asia instantly became frustrated. "Look, let's just drop it okay. I'm tired of talking about that."

Before Keon could respond his cell phone rang. Looking at the screen, he turned back to Asia. "Baby, this is business. Look in the other box with the bow, then get dressed in the next surprise. I'll meet you downstairs for dinner," he said, before jetting out the room.

"Damn, that must've been important," Asia said to herself. "I hope it's not some bitch because if so she might as well move the fuck on. He's mine now."

🏈🏈🏈🏈🏈🏈🏈

Seven o'clock the next morning, Asia woke up to the sound of the alarm on her cell phone. Reaching her hand over toward Keon's only nightstand, she was surprised that he wasn't beside her. However after the sudden smell of food lingered into the bedroom, it didn't take long to realize that he was cooking once again.

I love a man that can cook, she thought.

After the candle light dinner and sex marathon they had the night before, she wondered if Keon could be the one to finally make her settle down. Something no other man had been able to do.

Getting out of bed, Asia went to use the bathroom and frowned from the slight pain once she sat on the toilet. "Damn, it's been a long time since a man made my pussy sting like this." Moments later she smiled. "But I'll take this pain any day."

Thinking about their wild night of sex once again, Asia quickly wiped herself then jumped up before making her way downstairs. But as she approached the top step she heard Keon on the phone downstairs and stopped instantly at the mention

85

of her name.

She was curious to see what he was talking about. Her antennas went up immediately as Keon attempted to whisper. Little did he know, Asia had bionic ears and could hear almost anything after dealing with so many sneaky-ass men.

She eased down closer when she heard Keon say, "Trust me Sandino, Asia is about to tell me everything about her involvement and the whereabouts of Skye. I can handle her; she's eating out the palm of my hands. I'm going to take her out to dinner tonight...you know wine and dine her ass then get her tipsy so she'll start talking. I'll hit you back to-morrow," he said hanging up.

Asia felt sick to her stomach at the fact that Keon had crossed her and was working for Sandino. She ran back up-stairs to the bedroom.

A few seconds later, Asia heard him coming up the stairs and she ran into the bathroom closing the door and lock-ing it. She heard Keon calling her name.

"Asia, I got a surprise for you," he said carrying a tray with food. She saw the bathroom doorknob turning followed by a knock. "What's wrong baby?" he yelled through the door.

Asia didn't respond, but decided to open the door any-way.

"What's wrong, baby?" he asked.

"You crossed me," she responded.

Keon looked at her sideways. "What are you talking about?"

"Look, don't play fucking dumb with me."

When Keon realized Asia must've overheard his con-versation with Sandino, he quickly tried to plead his case.

"Fuck you Keon!" Asia yelled.

She rushed past him trying to grab her clothes, but did-n't get far before Keon grabbed her by the neck and slung her across the room.

Asia's eyes searched the room for her purse as he instantly changed into a different person. "You stupid bitch. We could've both made some money off Sandino's ass, but I see you don't wanna act right."

"I can't believe you would do this to me!" Asia yelled. "How could you talk to Sandino after the way he treated you at the party?"

"Easy. When Sandino called and told me about the money you and Skye stole from him, he told me that he would hire me back if I could find out some information from you. He thought I went along with it because I needed my job back. But I only went along with it to get his ass back. Fuck Sandino. I just want the money he was talking about," Keon informed.

Asia got up feeling a little dizzy, but reluctantly started taking off her clothes trying to think of a plan. She knew if she tried to fight chances of her wining were slim, so sex had to be her secret weapon.

Unfortunately her plan failed. Instead of getting horny, Keon grabbed Asia by the hair then pushed her over to the bed. Seconds later, he pushed his elbow into her chest.

"You need to tell me where the fuck the money is that y'all stole. I could care less where Skye is. She deserves better anyway," Keon said.

"I don't know what you're talking about. I swear!"

"Stop lying, bitch!"

With his hands wrapped tightly around her throat, Asia knew she had to do something before he killed her. Thinking fast, she quickly raised her leg then kneed him in the nuts as hard as she could. She jumped back as Keon hit the floor yelling out in pain. Seconds later, Asia took it upon herself to start kicking him several times as he balled up in a fetal position trying to avoid the blows from her continuous stomps. Several kicks later, she stepped over him and immediately gathered her things.

"I'm going to kill your ass, Asia. You'll never be able to

walk the streets for doing this to me," he yelled loudly.

Not taking his threats lightly, Asia reached for her purse on his desk then quickly pulled her black .32 caliber out. "What did you just say?" she questioned.

"I said I'm going to kill your ass," Keon replied. He was obviously not affected by the sight of the gun.

"Not if I kill your ass first," Asia said before pulling the trigger.

Noticing a small hole in his forehead, Asia watched his body jerk and the blood run out the side of his mouth. Seconds later, he stopped moving all together. Grabbing her towel from the night before, Asia franticly tried to wipe down everything she'd touched. Realizing her fingerprints were probably on everything in the condo, she quickly put back on her clothes then grabbed all her belongings before making a swift exit out of the door.

Walking nervously to her car, Asia constantly looked around to see if anyone was watching her before jumping inside and pulling off. Glancing around the parking lot one last time, when she finally made it to the street, Asia hit the accelerator and headed to her job with plans to get all the money and get the hell out of dodge. She always wanted to visit the windy city.

"Chicago, here I come!"

Chapter Twelve 🏈

A week passed since Skye had arrived at the shelter, and she still hadn't been able to reach Asia. Completely surprised that she'd changed her number, Skye then tried to reach Asia at her job, but was shocked to find out that she'd quit.

"Where the hell could that bitch be with my money? If I wasn't so scared to go back to Florida, I would go looking for her ass," Skye said to herself.

Her body began to shiver and her temper rose at the thought of Asia double crossing her. It was beyond foul and something Skye thought Asia would never do. "How the fuck am I gonna make it with three kids and no money?" Skye carried on. "I'm ready to get the hell out this shelter."

Shaking her head in disbelief, Skye looked at the clock on the dusty nightstand and realized that it was time for her counseling session with Justice. As an occupant in the shelter the only requirement that had to be met was meeting with him twice a week. However, in the few days she'd been there Skye also started exercising daily. Anything was better than sitting around thinking about Asia all day. She still stayed to herself and didn't mingle with the other ladies in the house. The last thing she needed right now was another shiesty bitch coming into her life. Besides, it was obvious that the other women didn't care too much for her. They'd made that known from the constant evil stares they gave her whenever Skye walked into a room. Luckily, she didn't care. As long as her sons were fitting in and nobody fucked with them everything was cool.

The only person Skye seemed to have a connection with was Justice. Unlike Sandino, Skye liked the fact that he was easy to talk to, and an even better listener. He'd also had a session with the boys, which seemed to help with Jordan, but Kareem had yet to open up. Although he was finally getting along with Joey and Manny, Kareem hadn't shown any signs of trusting another man.

Skye grabbed Payton and headed toward Justice's office for her session. However, before she could bend the corner, she noticed the big girl peeking out her room.

"Can you come here for a second? I need to talk to you real quick," the girl said.

Skye stopped and looked around, wondering if the girl was talking to her.

"I need to warn you about that bitch," the girl said waving her hand so Skye could come to her room.

Skye was hesitant about talking to her and damn sure wasn't going inside her room, especially since the big girl hadn't said two words to Skye since she'd arrived.

"I'm not gonna bite," the girl replied.

Skye walked in the direction of her room to see what she wanted. She stood at the door noticing all her belongings packed up and ready to go.

"What's your name again?" the girl asked.

"Janelle."

"Right…okay Janelle well I'm Toya."

They briefly shook hands.

"Listen honey, I been watching you, and you look like you smart, but I have to warn you about that bitch Mercedes. She's not to be trusted. She's missing a few screws inside that head of hers if you know what I mean. She's jealous of every woman who comes into the shelter that looks better than her. She needs to be in a crazy house not working here. Just watch your back when it comes to her ass!"

A few seconds later, Mercedes came walking past them and instead of speaking, she rolled her eyes instead.

"See what I mean," Toya replied.

"Yeah…thanks," Skye said before walking away.

She'd actually noticed how strange Mercedes had been acting lately, which made Skye wonder if it really did have something to do with the comfortable relationship between her and Justice. She got the impression that Mercedes might've had a thing for him, but didn't feel comfortable enough getting into either of their business. Little did Mercedes know, Skye couldn't allow herself to get involved with another man right now. She just really enjoyed his company nonetheless. In the meantime Mercedes would just have to accept the newfound friendship

Minutes later, Skye knocked on the door to Justice's office.

"Come in!" he yelled.

When Skye turned the knob and walked inside, Justice was sitting behind the desk looking fine as ever.

"Hey Janelle, how are you? Are you feeling better since we met the other day?"

"Yeah, I'm feeling a little better."

He looked at Payton as she turned to him and smiled at the sound of his voice. "So, have you thought about what we discussed?"

"Yes, I did some thinking and I'm ready to open up and discuss the abuse."

"Good, that's what I wanted to hear. You can start whenever you're ready."

Skye took a deep breath. "My husband who I would rather not disclose his name has been abusing me for years. I put up with it and made excuses because I didn't want to give up the lifestyle my kids and I were accustomed to. I also didn't want to break up my family. But after the beatings got out of hand, I did attempt to leave on a few occasions, but always went back after he promised to get help and do better."

"That's what most men say," Justice informed.

"After he hit me even though we had a house full of people this last time, I couldn't take it anymore. I had to leave; I didn't want my boy's growing up thinking it was okay to beat women. I've already seen abusive behavior in my son Kareem." Skye was still too embarrassed to talk about the rape. "It's amazing what can happen when you give a man control over your life."

"It was good that you got out Janelle," Justice replied in a soft tone.

"I should've left a long time ago."

"Did you ever try and call the police after one of the incidents?"

"Are you crazy? He would've killed me for sure if I'd done that." Skye looked down then ran her hand through Payton's soft, curly hair. "Things got ten times worse when I got pregnant with my daughter. He didn't want me to have her."

"Did he beat you while you were pregnant?"

Suddenly a tear raced down Skye's cheek. "For the first three months. He was so pissed off that I decided to keep the baby," she said after wiping her face. "Can you believe he even insisted on naming her when she was born? How crazy is that?"

Justice looked at Skye. "Janelle I'm glad you feel comfortable enough to open up more, just know that you can trust me." When Skye nodded her head, Justice gave her a sincere look. "Can I ask you a really personal question?"

"I guess."

"How old are you?"

"Thirty-four…why?" Skye inquired.

"Because you don't look a day over twenty-five." Justice also wanted to tell Skye how beautiful she was, but decided against it.

"Thanks." It was hard for Skye to accept the compliment since she'd managed to let Sandino lower her self esteem.

"Janelle, you're safe here. It's time for you to start over and look out for yourself. You're a great mother. Most women aren't strong enough to leave, but you put your kids first and that says a lot about you."

"I can't thank you enough for all your help, Justice. I'm so glad to be free and have control of my own life."

Skye felt the tears building up once again. Soon they were flowing down her face. At that moment, Justice went against the rules by walking over to Skye and giving her a hug. He couldn't deny her beauty or his attraction to her as she cried on his shoulder. Both of them were so embraced in the hug, they didn't notice Mercedes standing in the door way.

"What the hell are you doing, Justice?" Mercedes questioned with a cigarette in her hand.

Justice looked up. "What have I told you about smoking inside the house? There's a designated area outside for that."

Mercedes took a short puff. "The hell with that, I've been having a stressful day. But don't try and change the subject. What are you doing?"

"This is none of your concern, Mercedes. Mind your business and close the door behind you," Justice responded.

"What do you mean it's none of my concern? That shit is against the rules. Are you willing to jeopardize all that we've built here for her?" Mercedes replied.

Skye wiped her tears away as Justice walked toward the door. "*We've* built? Are you serious? Go put that damn cigarette out," he said, before closing the door. After walking back to his desk and sitting down, Justice continued. "Sorry about that Janelle. Mercedes can be so unprofessional at times. Anyway, our Domestic Violence Program will help you move, find a place to live, a job and get on your feet."

Skye looked at Justice knowing he was right; she had to

get a job and support her family. She couldn't stay at the shelter forever, especially since she couldn't keep Kareem and Jordan out of school much longer.

Once their session was over Skye went back to her room and put Payton to sleep. Afterwards she laid across the bed thinking about the hug she shared with Justice. She couldn't seem to get it out of her mind, his arms felt so good, so safe...so right.

Instantly, her vision on their embrace was quickly erased when her sons came running in the room telling her to come look at the T.V. Skye had no idea why they were so emotional and pulling her down the hall in such a hurry.

When they reached the family room and saw Sandino's picture posted next to the Channel 5 news anchor, her eyes widened.

"Sandino Washington, a Defensive Tackle for the Miami Dolphins was arrested last night on a gun possession and aggravated assault charges after a shooting that occurred in a South Beach night club, and has resulted in one injury. Stay tuned for more details."

As soon as the news went off, Skye and the boys realized that they couldn't react or show any emotions while other people were around. They listened as one of the women made a comment about how she couldn't understand why pro ball players and celebrities made all the money and still got arrested for doing stupid shit.

Moments later, Skye, Kareem and Jordan headed outside and walked toward the front yard. In complete shock, the boys stood speechless.

"Can't we go home now?' Kareem asked.

"No, we can never go back home Kareem," Skye answered.

Kareem shrugged his shoulders. "Why not, he's locked up and can't hit you anymore."

"Because he might post bail and get right back out. I

can't take that chance."

Clearly upset, Kareem stormed back inside. Jordan on the other hand could care less.

"I never want to see him again anyway. I hope they throw away the key," Jordan said. He kissed his mother on the cheek before walking back inside as well.

Skye knew Sandino's high price lawyer would probably get him off, but she couldn't help but smirk when thoughts of him being behind bars invaded her thoughts. *Maybe this is a sign that things might just go my way after all.*

As Skye continued to walk around outside, little did she know Mercedes had entered her room without permission. Mercedes puffed on her cigarette as she walked over to Payton asleep on the bed and stood over her. She brushed her hands threw Payton's hair.

"What a cute baby. Too bad she belongs to that bitch," Mercedes said, blowing smoke. She removed the blanket. "Wonder how upset that bitch would be if I..."

Looking back to see if anyone was coming, Mercedes tapped the cigarette causing hot ashes to fall on Payton's bare leg. Before she could start wailing, Mercedes quickly covered her mouth.

"Ssshhhh be quiet. It couldn't have hurt that bad."

No sooner than Mercedes removed her hand, Skye walked back into the room. When she saw Mercedes leaning over her baby with the cigarette, she went crazy.

"Why the hell are you in my room?" Skye asked. When she noticed ashes on Payton's leg, she was infuriated. "Did you pluck fucking ashes on my baby? Bitch, are you crazy? Did you try to burn her?" She quickly picked Payton up.

"Ain't nobody touch your precious baby. The ashes must've fallen by accident. She was crying, so I came to help your ass out. Who leaves a baby unattended?" Mercedes turned around and walked toward the door.

After laying Payton back down on the bed, Skye

walked up behind Mercedes and pushed her on the floor. "Don't you ever put your fucking hands on any of my kids!"

"Bitch, you're gonna regret putting your damn hands on me," Mercedes said jumping up. She dove on Skye and they locked onto one another like two pit bulls.

Mercedes swung hitting Skye in the face several times. Skye then jumped on top of her and put her in the choke hold. With visions of Sandino beating her all over again, she completely lost it. She started choking Mercedes until Justice ran into the room.

"What the hell is going on, break it up ladies!" he demanded.

He attempted to pull them apart, but Skye grabbed a chunk of Mercedes hair and tried to rip her scalp out.

"Tell this bitch to let go of my hair Justice!" Mercedes pleaded.

"Janelle please, there's a no fighting policy at the shelter," Justice responded.

At that moment, Skye let go. She didn't want Mercedes to be the cause of her family getting kicked out.

"This shit ain't over," Mercedes said, leaving her room.

Chapter Thirteen 🏈

4 Months Later

Shortly after 1:00 am Skye heard a loud pounding sound at the front door. She jumped out of bed and grabbed the baby before quickly proceeding down the hall. By the time she made it to Jordan and Kareem's room they'd already ran out wondering what was going on as well. Despite months of a peaceful household, the entire family was still on edge.

"How did he find us? Isn't he still in jail?" Jordan asked. It didn't take much for everyone to know who he was talking about.

Skye didn't know what to think as the banging continued. "Oh my God Kareem, did you call him? Did you tell him where we were?" she yelled. "How could you?"

Before he could answer, someone yelled, "Cobb County Police! Open the door now!"

As her eyes increased, a part of Skye was relived that it wasn't Sandino while the other half still questioned what they wanted. Hesitantly, she walked over and opened her apartment door. Within seconds, her small, barely furnished living room was swarming with four officers wearing dark blue police jackets.

"Get on the floor now!" one of the white officers yelled with his gun drawn. With dirty blonde hair and thick eyebrows, he reminded Skye of Justin Timberlake.

"What's going on?" Skye screamed while her sons instantly dropped to the floor. Before she had time to ask anything else, they were handcuffed behind their backs.

Moments later, a female office appeared and took Payton out of Skye's hands as she was forced to the floor and handcuffed as well.

"This is a beautiful baby. Too bad she has to live in a home like this," the female officer said in a sarcastic tone.

"A home like what? What are you talking about?" Skye questioned.

"Ma'am we have reason to believe there are drugs inside this residence," another officer responded. Unlike the Justin knockoff, he was slightly overweight.

Skye frowned. "Drugs? Oh no, you must have the wrong apartment, we just moved here a few months ago. You must be looking for the people who used to live here before us or something. There must be a mistake."

"We know how long you've lived here. Trust me, we know *everything* that goes on in this neighborhood," the chubby officer informed.

He placed a search warrant down in front of Skye's face. She tired to look up at the paperwork, but everything seemed to be a blur.

Skye laid handcuffed on the floor as they proceeded to search the apartment. She then looked over at her sons. Jordan had a scared expression on his face while Kareem had a guilty expression on his. He turned his head when he saw Skye looking in his direction.

"Do either of you know what's going on?" Skye tried to whisper. However, the female officer quickly told her to be quiet.

Skye watched as the officers tore the apartment inside, out. They searched every room, every piece of furniture, and even dismantled Payton's crib.

"This is crazy!" Skye yelled franticly.

At that moment, the overweight officer helped Skye up off the floor and removed her cuffs. He then walked over to Jordan, helped him up and removed his as well.

Skye thought they were gonna remove Kareem's next until a black guy with bad acne and an old, dingy, Rocawear sweat shirt walked into the apartment and headed straight toward her oldest son.

"Do you remember me?" he asked.

Kareem looked at the officer and lowered his head.

"Don't be shy now, son," the officer continued. "We just met each other yesterday. You couldn't have forgotten me that fast."

When Kareem still didn't respond, the pimpled face officer helped him up, then politely told him that he was under arrest.

Kareem instantly looked at Skye, but never said a word.

"Are you serious? He's not a drug dealer. He wouldn't dare have drugs in this house!" Skye shouted.

"Well, I'm afraid you're wrong because we found this inside the sock drawer of your son's room," the blonde haired officer chimed in. He held up what looked like two ounces of cooked crack cocaine. It was already bagged in 20's. "The room with the bunk bed's...that is his room, right?"

Skye's heart rate increased when she realized that drugs had been found in her home. "Yes, but..."

The blonde officer cut her off. "That's what we thought."

When the officer continued to escort Kareem toward the door, she lost it. "My son can't go to jail, he has school tomorrow!"

"Ma'am your son should've thought about that before he sold drugs to an undercover cop," Mr. Acne replied.

Skye was floored. She couldn't believe what he'd just blurted out. "Are y'all at least gonna let him put on some pants and shoes?" Skye managed to say as Kareem walked outside with only a t-shirt and basketball shorts on.

The cold, brisk January air was well under forty.

"I'm sure he'll be issued some flip flops," the female officer stated as she handed Payton back.

"What's going to happen to my son?" Skye questioned with tears in her eyes. "Where are you taking him?"

"He'll be transported to the Marietta Youth Detention Center since he's under age," the female officer informed her.

At that point all Skye could do was shake her head as she watched the officer's escort her oldest son out of the house and place him in the back of a police car.

Once the car pulled off, Skye grabbed her prepaid cell phone. *Is this how the new year is going to start*, she thought. "Justice, I need you!" Skye screamed in the phone when he answered.

🏈🏈🏈🏈🏈🏈🏈

Skye looked around her trashed apartment in complete disbelief. After staying in the shelter for another month after Sandino got locked up, she was happy when Justice was finally able to help her find a job along with her current home in Marietta, Georgia. Although the two bedroom apartment wasn't as fabulous as her Miami mansion, Skye was proud to call the place her own. Even though Justice bought her a few pieces of furniture for Christmas and had even given her some items out of his personal home and the shelter, Skye couldn't wait until she saved enough money to buy another T.V, and a dining room set. Eating at wooden fold-out tables had already taken its toll on them.

When they first moved in, it took a while for everybody to get used to living in a cramped space and a neighborhood full of Spanish people. They'd gone from a spotless home to a place where they saw an occasional roach, but it would just have to do until Skye got on her feet. She and Jordan dealt with it, but Kareem didn't like living there at all. He started staying out all night and even skipped school a few times, but always assured Skye he would get his act together whenever she went off. Up until now, Skye was happy that she had a piece of mind, but apparently Kareem was going to be her next problem. She knew he'd been hanging with some of the local neighborhood boys, but she never thought in a million years that he would get in trouble for selling drugs. He was definitely turning into someone she barely knew.

She often wondered if Sandino was still locked up. Not knowing the circumstances, Skye prayed that he never saw the streets again, so she could really move on with her life comfortably. She asked Kareem almost everyday if he'd talked to his father again. She feared that since Kareem was so rebellious right now, he might end up calling Sandino, but each time her son promised her that he hadn't. Skye just hoped Kareem's word could be trusted.

Skye glanced at the oak wood dresser and all the drawers that had been pulled out, when her mind suddenly drifted to Justice. Remembering when he and his cousin helped move the furniture inside, she thought about how Justice had really been there for her and the kids since they moved in. Skye also couldn't deny the fact that she missed seeing him at the shelter everyday and was really starting to like him.

As Skye continued to think, Justice knocked on the door five minutes later. After asking who it was, Jordan slowly opened the door, then walked back to the couch with a sad look on his face.

"She's in her bedroom," was all he said.

Justice looked around the house. "What happened? Is everything okay?"

Jordan just shrugged his shoulders and continued watching T.V while Justice walked off. He headed down the hall past the boy's room noticing that it had been completely ransacked. Both twin mattresses were off the bunk beds and clothes were scattered all over the floor. Wondering what happened since Skye refused to tell him over the phone, he knocked on her bedroom door.

"Who is it?"

"It's me, Justice."

Skye placed her newly cut hair behind her eyes. She'd finally retired the wig. "Come in."

When he walked inside, Justice watched as Skye placed a pair of shoes back inside her closet then glance at Payton who was on the bare mattress asleep. He could tell Skye had been crying.

"Did somebody break in here? Where's Kareem? Talk to me," he grabbed Skye and hugged her.

She instantly crumbled in his arms. "The police came to the house looking for Kareem. They found drugs in his room."

"What?" Justice asked in shock.

"They arrested him. I need to go bail him out, but you know I don't have that type of money," Skye informed.

"Don't worry about that, I got you," Justice replied.

"Where did they take him?"

"To some detention center."

"There's only one in Marietta. I know where it is, let's go," Justice quickly replied.

After grabbing her purse, Skye called and asked her neighbor Lydia, who lived on the first floor if Jordan and Payton could come over and stay with her while she ran out. She was Payton's babysitter and also came over and tutored Jordan on his Spanish sometimes, so Skye knew that after giving the woman twenty dollars the fact that it was after two a.m. didn't matter. Lydia was also nosey so Skye was sure that her neighbor knew exactly where she was going.

After Lydia agreed, Skye told Jordan to get Payton ready and head downstairs until they got back. He didn't really want to go, but Skye told him it wasn't safe for them to be there alone. Jordan sighed, but unlike Kareem he also listened to what his mother said.

When they left her apartment a few minutes later, Justice who always insisted on opening the car door helped Skye inside his black BMW 760 LI, then pulled off.

Skye glanced around his car thinking, *nobody really drives 7 series BMW's like this anymore. They're old, but then again I'm driving a fucking Honda now so who am I to talk?* Skye couldn't wait to get rid of the car which legally wasn't hers. She couldn't help but wonder if the cook back at the diner was actually driving around in her Jag.

While riding, Skye was in a zone as she looked out the window thinking how any of this could've happened.

Justice gently placed his hand on her leg. "It'll be okay. I have a lot of connections with some good lawyers. We'll get Kareem off."

"Justice, how could my own son be selling drugs and I not even notice it? I mean…I did notice him outside hanging around crazy-looking boys sometimes; you know this isn't a good neighborhood. But I gave him his space because their father never allowed them to have many friends. When I found out he was skipping school and when he stayed out all night, I thought I'd put my foot down, but apparently not. Kareem is so mad at me because he wants to get his license, but I won't let him."

"Well, you should let him get his license, what harm would that be?" Justice asked. "Are you afraid that your husband will try and find you?"

At that moment Skye contemplated about telling Justice who she really was, but decided against it. She still wasn't ready. "Actually I am. Things are okay the way they are right now," Skye replied. "Furthermore, it's only been a few months since we've been gone."

When she suddenly started crying, Justice rubbed her legs again. "I know what you're thinking…it's not your fault. You're doing a great job, look at Jordan."

Skye wiped away a few tears. "Yeah, he's the perfect son. He doesn't give me any problems, and always helps out around the house. He's also doing well in school."

"See...everything will be okay. Besides, I'm here now so you don't have to be alone anymore," he assured. "Oh, by the way I've been meaning to tell you, I'm so glad you stopped wearing that wig. The *real you*, is so much more beautiful.'

Skye couldn't help but blush as Justice turned on County Services Parkway and pulled up at the facility a few minutes later.

"Wait let me get that door for you," Justice said, jumping out and running to her side of the car.

"Thanks," Skye replied after getting out.

She had to get use to a man being respectable to her again. She really could open her own door, but it felt good every time he did it.

Once they walked inside, Justice saw an officer sitting at the front desk. They rushed over to him.

"Excuse me sir, we need to find out some information on Kareem Coleman."

Skye couldn't help but chuckle when Justice blurted out the fake last name.

The officer keyed the name into the computer. "We do have a Kareem in the system, but we have him down as Kareem Doe because he refused to give us his last name and he was arrested without any ID."

Skye nodded her head. "Yes, I'm sure that's him."

"Has he been charged?' Justice asked.

"Yes, he's been charged with procession of crack cocaine. Apparently Joey and Manny Guzman were charged and brought in with him for the same thing."

"Joey and Manny, those are Mercedes' sons. I knew those boys weren't shit," Justice said. "I'd like to bail Kareem out."

"Since its Sunday he'll have to wait until the morning

to appear in front of the judge. Bail can't be posted until then sir," the officer informed.

Skye sighed and dropped her head.

Will he be at the Juvenile Court, sir?" Justice inquired.

"How old is Kareem?" the officer asked.

"He just turned seventeen a few weeks ago," Skye informed.

"No, anyone seventeen and older has to appear at the regular court building on Waddell Street. Court sessions start at 10:00 a.m. Do you know where it is?" the officer asked.

"Yes, I do, thanks," Justice responded.

Suddenly, they heard the sound of high heels clicking on the concrete floor. When Justice and Skye looked back, Mercedes walked up to the front desk. The three immediately locked eyes on one another.

"What the hell are you doing here?" Mercedes asked Justice. She was all dolled up like she'd just been pulled out of the club wearing a short, black skin-tight dress and a pair of black five-inch thigh high boots.

"We're here because your fucking drug dealing sons were obviously a bad influence on my son while we were staying in the shelter!" Skye yelled.

"Bitch, nobody put a gun to your precious son's head. That boy ain't right anyway, so don't blame my boys because he wants to sling drugs," Mercedes shot back.

"I got your bitch right here," Skye said walking toward Mercedes.

Justice jumped between both women as the officer stood up. "Please take that outside!" the officer demanded.

Mercedes rolled her eyes at the officer and kept talking. "Justice, answer my question. What the fuck are you doing here? You didn't even bother to ask if I was okay. You've been neglecting me and your duties at the shelter for a few weeks now. Don't tell me it's because of her ass?"

"Mercedes, mind your business. I don't owe you any

explanations for why I'm here with Janelle. Go take care of your sons. If you'd been doing that from the beginning none of this shit would be happening right now," Justice responded. "Come on, let's go Janelle."

After walking out of the station, Justice opened the car door for Skye before hopping into the driver's side. He was just about to pull off when Mercedes jumped in front of the car and just stood there with her hands on her hips.

Justice blew the horn. When she didn't move, he rolled down the window. "Mercedes, get the hell out the way before I hit your stupid ass!"

As soon as Mercedes moved to the side, Justice's tires screeched as he quickly drove past her and headed to the parking lot exit.

"You're gonna regret fucking with me!" Mercedes yelled.

Chapter Fourteen

Justice watched as the sun crept through Skye's apartment window. He'd been propped up against the headboard in his clothes for hours looking at how beautiful Skye was as she slept. With Skye so upset over Kareem's arrest, Justice insisted on staying with her and they ended up falling asleep in each other's arms. He enjoyed every minute of his first night laying next to her. Moving the sheet, he rubbed his hands across her arms noticing several old scars. He wondered how she along with all the other women he counseled could have such pleasant spirits after being abused for so many years. Nevertheless he planned to make sure nobody ever hurt Skye again and would protect her by any means necessary. When he reached over and kissed her on the forehead, she opened her eyes and looked at him.

"What time is? Why are you sitting up in the bed?" she asked.

"Its 7:30 a.m. I've been admiring how beautiful you are."

When Skye realized the scars on her arms were exposed, she quickly grabbed the sheet and pulled it back up.

"You don't have to hide your body, baby," Justice said, pulling her close.

Skye wanted to melt in his arms. She snuggled up close to his chest and wrapped her arms around his as Justice started kissing on her neck. A chill ran through her body. It was almost as if he knew that was her hot spot. Skye was hesitant because Jordan and Payton were just down the hall, but couldn't resist his touch. She looked in the direction of her closed bedroom door as Justice continued giving her soft pecks. He was so gentle, so passionate, and so different from Sandino. Skye closed her eyes as he moved downward and kissed her lips. She became wet instantly.

"Let me show you how you deserved to be treated," Justice whispered in her ear then kissed her lobe.

Even though Skye's heart said no, her body definitely said yes. At that moment, Justice reached down and unzipped her jeans and slid them off as well as her panties. He stood up on the side of the bed and quickly stepped out his clothes, then reached down and grabbed a condom out of his pocket and slid it on. As Justice threw the wrapper on the nightstand, Skye couldn't help but sneak a quick look.

He's using Magnums...thank God, she thought before admiring his body. He wasn't necessarily cut up like LL Cool J, but his ten and a half inch dick certainly made up for what he lacked.

With her pussy soaking wet by now, Skye stretched across the bed slightly elevating her back. It had been awhile since she had a man really make love to her.

Justice climbed back into bed and gently opened her legs before positioning himself between her thighs. He continued to plant warm, wet kisses on her skin while staring into her eyes. Anxiously, he slid his stiff huge dick inside her wetness causing Skye to squirm. Justice moved deeper inside her with his slow smooth motion.

"You're so big," she moaned.

"I'm not hurting you am I?"

"No baby, you feel good."

"Damn, you feel good, too," he whispered with an expression of ecstasy on his face.

Suddenly, Justice started pumping faster and harder while watching Skye as she grabbed her taupe colored sheets with pleasure.

"Fuck me, baby," Skye purred.

It was the first time in years that she'd actually been vocal during a sexual experience. Sex with Sandino normally led to her crying since he was always so aggressive.

"Awww…it feels so good."

Skye's soft voice gave Justice immediate satisfaction. He tried his best to hold back, but couldn't. His body stiffened.

"Dammm," he groaned while unloading thick white cum into the rubber.

At the same time, Skye felt her pussy walls jumping as she reached her climax and released her juices all over his thick dick. Both seemed to be in complete heaven as Justice fell back on the bed and smiled. Glancing at the clock, Skye realized that she had at least an hour to chill before getting up to go see about Kareem. She laid her naked body up against his chest as Justice wrapped his big strong arms around her body. She felt so safe.

I could really get used to this, she thought.

🏈🏈🏈🏈🏈🏈🏈🏈

Justice's good mood was completely blown as they stood in the lobby of The Cobb County Court talking with a local bail bondsman. Since it was Kareem's first offense, the judge lowered his bail to three thousand at his arraignment earlier that morning. Agreeing to pay the ten percent, Justice had already given the bondsman, who obviously spent way too much time at the tanning salon, a credit card, but things weren't going according to plan.

"Can you run it again?" Justice questioned.

"Mr. Mitchell, I've already ran it twice. Both times were declined. Do you have another card?" the bondsman asked.

Justice couldn't believe the bondsman kept a portable machine in his briefcase. Slightly embarrassed, he reached in his wallet and pulled out another card, praying this card would work. Skye looked at him strange wondering why he would offer to help if he really didn't have the money. The bondsman swiped the second card.

"Okay this one went through," he said, passing Justice his card back.

Justice breathed a sigh of relief.

"Maybe you need to call your bank for the other one. I'm sure it's just a minor mistake," the bondsman added.

"I sure will," Justice replied. He signed the small piece of paper.

"You can head back over to the Detention Center. He's gonna be released there," the bondsman informed before handing Justice his receipt and walking away.

After making the short, three mile trip and into a small, crowded waiting area, Justice and Skye sat for what seemed like hours for Kareem to be released. The loud screams from several unruly children almost gave Skye a migraine along with the crazy, braless woman who kept yelling that they needed to release her son now! For a Juvenile Detention Center, the place was a mad house.

Justice picked up Skye's hand and kissed it. "How do you feel about the judge placing Kareem on house arrest until his court date?"

"Even if I was pissed, there's nothing I can do about it. I am pissed that he has to be home schooled now. The judge could've at least made that exception."

"Well, I'm sure he has his reasons. Maybe he knows Kareem is a good kid and just wants him off the streets," Justice replied in a sincere tone.

"But this is his first offense. And it's his senior year."

"Yeah I know, but honestly it's for his own good. Don't worry though. I know a lawyer who plays golf with damn near all the Cobb County judges. I should be able to do something."

Skye finally smiled. "I don't know how to thank you for all you've done. I never even thanked you for those fake school transcripts you got me."

"Don't worry, you thanked me enough this morning," Justice replied.

This time, they both smiled.

A few minutes later, Justice stood up from the hard chair. Getting a little impatient, he was ready to leave so he could go back home and freshen up, but didn't want Skye to think he wasn't being supportive. He walked to the water fountain and got a sip of water. When Justice turned around he bumped into a tall guy standing directly behind him.

"Oh, excuse me man. I didn't see you." Justice assured.

The guy looked at him long and hard. "Don't I know you nigga?"

Justice looked at him trying to see if he knew the guy from somewhere. "Naw, I'm afraid not."

"Trust me, I never forget a face. You the mutherfucka who beat me and my boys out of three g's in a crap game a few years ago over by Bankhead Courts."

"You must have me mixed up with someone else. I don't play craps," Justice said, as he walked away.

The guy continued staring at Justice as he returned to the waiting area and sat down beside Skye.

"Who was that?"

"I have no idea," Justice quickly replied.

Finally after another twenty-five minutes passed, Kareem was released. He smiled when he saw Skye, but immediately noticed the disappointed and mad expression on her face. An expression he knew oh so well. He walked over and hugged her neck knowing she was fed up with him and his rebellious ways.

"I'm sorry I messed up, Ma. I just wanted to make some money so you wouldn't have to work at that job you just got."

"So, that's your excuse for…" Skye lowered her voice when she realized that she was yelling. "For trying to sell fucking crack. I can't believe this." She stared down at his leg. "Do you realize that you have on a monitoring bracelet now? That shit ain't cute. You're a damn criminal now."

"I just made a bad mistake, but I'm not a criminal."

"You have a record now, so that does make your ass a criminal," she fired back. "You smoking that shit, too?"

Kareem shook his head. "Absolutely not."

"What about weed?" Skye questioned.

Kareem seemed to be at a loss for words for a moment. "No, I would never do that."

"Yeah right. You probably lying, but you better hope I don't catch your ass doing that shit."

"I know, Ma. Thanks for getting me out."

"Don't' thank me, thank Justice. He put up the bail money."

With a frown on his face, Kareem instantly got upset when he saw Justice walk up. He never said a word.

"Did you hear what I just said? Thank Justice for getting you out!" Skye yelled. Kareem just stood there.

"You know what, you're stubborn, just like your fucking father!"

"Its cool Janelle, he doesn't have to thank me," Justice responded.

"Can we leave now, *Janelle*?" Kareem asked.

Realizing that the Detention Center wasn't the place to smack the shit out of her son, Skye stormed toward the door with her lips poked out. She couldn't wait to get home and curse Kareem out for putting her through unnecessary stress. She was sick of his immature and ungrateful-ass attitude.

❦❦❦❦❦❦❦

The car ride home was silent. Skye looked out the window wondering if she could juggle a relationship with Justice and focus on her sons at the same time. She deserved to have a life, but her sons obviously needed her attention more than a man did right now. She could tell being displaced from their home was really starting to take its toll on Kareem. His behavior was becoming more out of control by the minute.

As soon as they got back home, Skye instantly jumped into Kareem's shit. He tuned her out most of the time, but did manage to hear when she told him that he had to get his act together, and to stop being so disrespectful. She even told him that his attitude was just like Sandino's.

"Well, let me go back and live with him then. He's getting out soon anyway!"

Skye's eyes enlarged. Not only did she not want him talking reckless in front of Justice, but she also couldn't believe what he'd just said. "How do you know when your father is getting out?" she questioned.

"Because I talked to him the other day," Kareem admitted.

Skye instantly went ballistic and started pacing the floor like a mental patient. "How the fuck did you talk to him?"

"He called me," Kareem stated.

"How? How did he get your *new* cell phone number?" Skye asked

"Because I called Black to see when my father was getting out and he must've given it to him," Kareem replied.

Skye was so mad, her body began to shake. "I can't believe you. Those bullshit- ass pre paid cell phones are supposed to be for emergencies only, and you turn around and call the fucking enemy! What the hell is wrong with you? Are you crazy? You can't talk to anybody he knows, especially Black! They'll find out where we are. Your father is crazy. Don't you understand that?" Skye began pacing again. "Did you tell him where we were?"

"I don't care, I'm tired of hiding!" Kareem yelled.

Skye slapped him across his face. "Did you tell him?"

Kareem hesitated for a moment. "No!"

Skye wasn't sure if she could believe her son. "I'm trying to make a better life for us and you're ruining it. I don't know you anymore. You aren't the son I raised. I should've left your ass in jail!"

"I hope you're not trying to make a new life with him," Kareem said, pointing to Justice.

Skye was so embarrassed. She told Kareem to apologize, but he just looked at her with a blank stare.

"Look, you're in my house. You're gonna respect Justice when he's here, you got that?"

"Yeah," Kareem said in a nonchalant tone, then walked to him and Jordan's room and slammed the door.

Kareem was so upset with his mother. As far as he was concerned he didn't think she was emotionally or mentally ready to start dating again. He especially didn't trust Justice. He didn't feel his intentions were honorable. He was sure he was playing on his mother's vulnerability and vowed to get him out of their lives as soon as possible before she fell in love with him.

Chapter Fifteen

Sandino shook his leg continuously while listening to his lawyer and agent during a visit about his release.

"I was able to get you off due to lack of evidence. As it turns out, the three witnesses at the night club who came forward in the beginning refuse to cooperate with authorities now. With the young man who was injured not actually seeing you fire the weapon, the district attorney felt as though he wouldn't have a case. It also helped that your gun was registered and you have a license to carry a concealed weapon. All of that worked in your favor," the Jewish man informed.

"It took your ass long enough. I've been in this jail, seventeen fuckin' weeks! S-e-v-e-n-t-e-e-n," Sandino reiterated. "I couldn't even go to my mother's funeral last month. I bet if I was one of them white quarterback muthafuckas I woulda been out by now!"

"Mr. Washington these things take time. Just be thankful that we were finally able to get the charges dropped," his lawyer responded.

Little do you know, my man Black was gettin' ready to take the charge for me if you hadn't come through, Sandino thought.

"They're preparing your paper work so you can be released tomorrow morning."

"Tomorrow morning?" Sandino asked in disbelief.

"Yes, that was the best I could do." His lawyer placed a few pieces of paper inside his briefcase. "I hope you'll stay out of trouble after all this."

Sandino frowned. "What difference would it make if I didn't? As long as you gettin' paid, why the fuck should you care?"

"As long as you sign the checks, I really don't care. I was just trying to give you some free legal advice," the lawyer responded in a sarcastic tone.

Sandino looked at the freckled face white man, wanting to throw a Mike Tyson style haymaker, but knew he wouldn't get out if he did. Instead, he turned to his agent.

"So, Bryan, have any other teams expressed interest in me? I'm ready to get back on that field next season."

Immediately after getting locked up, the Miami Dolphins dropped Sandino from the team. Apparently he had no idea about the clause in his contract that stated Sandino would be released if he was ever involved in any criminal activity. His former agent had failed to mention that to him as well.

"Sandino, nobody wants to touch you because of your temper. Hell, did you forget that you were suspended for that illegal hit during the pre-season? Most general managers won't even take my call because they know exactly what I want. Not to mention, you're one of the oldest Defensive Tackle's in the league. Everybody thinks you should retire anyway," Bryan replied.

Sandino banged his fist against the table. "Fuck what everybody else thinks. I'll retire when I'm good and goddamn ready! All them hatin' muthafuckas can go to hell, includin' you Bryan. Who's side are you on anyway?"

Bryan lowered his voice. "You were extremely intoxicated when you were arrested. That won't sit well with team owners right now. Maybe you should think about going to rehab and getting yourself together once you get out."

Sandino eyebrows crinkled. "Rehab, are you fuckin'

kiddin' me? I'm not doin' that shit."

"Why not? I know you've been in here for a while, but going to rehab, might be like a sign of good faith…to show that you're trying to change," Bryan lectured.

"Fuck that dumb shit," Sandino quickly replied.

"Well, if the press ever finds out that Skye took the kids and left that'll look even worse," Bryan added.

A vein in Sandino's neck started to pulsate. "That shit is temporary. My wife will be back home as soon as I get out of here! White players go through shit like this all the time," he said, standing up. "Bryan, I'm givin' your ass a week to find me a fuckin' team or it's curtains for you."

The guard walked over to the table. "Do we have a problem here?" he asked. "Mr. Washington, did you just threaten him?"

"Oh, no everything is fine," Sandino's lawyer assured the guard. He quickly gave Sandino a look that said, "please calm down."

Sandino stared back at the guard. "Yeah, chill the fuck out, everything is fine."

"You've gotta get a grip of your temper," Bryan advised.

"Have you had any luck findin' my wife? Did you look in the Atlanta area like I told you to?" Sandino asked his attorney.

"Sandino, I've been so busy trying to get you out, I haven't had time to deal with that issue. Besides, I'm not a private investigator. Maybe you should think about getting one if you're expecting some better results."

"Wit' the amount of money I pay both y'all muthafuckas, you'll be whatever the fuck I tell you to be! And I better have a fuckin' limo waitin' for me when I get outta this bitch! You hear me Bryan?" Sandino yelled.

"Yes, but please calm down," Bryan replied. "Yelling isn't gonna solve anything."

"I think we're all done here, I'll be in touch," his lawyer said, getting up to leave.

His agent shook his head. "Okay Sandino, remember to keep your mouth closed in regards to talking to the press tomorrow. If there's any chance of you getting back into the league, saying something stupid wouldn't be a good thing to do right now. I'll call you once you're released and get settled. Until then, lay low and keep your nose clean."

"Yeah, yeah," Sandino mumbled.

Once everyone was gone, Sandino waited for the guard to come and cuff him.

How the fuck did my life end up like this? I had it all, a career, lots of friends, a beautiful wife, kids, we were set for life. I still can't believe Skye would do this shit to me. At my lowest point too! After I got arrested I expected her to come back for support, but I guess I was wrong. Now that bitch is gonna be sorry she ever fucked wit' me.

🏈🏈🏈🏈🏈🏈🏈🏈

When Sandino was released from Dade County jail the next day, just as Bryan had predicted there were news reporters and photographers everywhere. They all seemed to ask the same question, what were his plans now that he was no longer in the league.

"Mr. Washington…Mr. Washington, how was it in jail? Everyone is dying to know what your daily routine was," one reporter boldly stated. "Did the inmates treat you like a celebrity?

"Are you afraid this experience will ruin your career?" another reporter blurted out.

Taking his agent's advice, Sandino jumped in the limo and told the driver to take him to Liberty City, instead of making a statement. When the driver looked at him through the rearview mirror, wondering why a former pro football player wanted to go to the hood, Sandino smiled.

"I'm in desperate need of some pussy right now, partner," Sandino admitted.

Not wanting to pry any further, the driver nodded his head and blew his horn trying to get past the reporters and the mob of people standing in the way.

"Run them muthafuckas ova if you have to, and turn that shit up!" Sandino yelled then bobbed his head to a new Fabolous song.

"Girl you be killin' 'em…you be killin' em," he repeated along with the chipped tooth rapper.

Knowing that Black laughed every time he danced, Sandino was glad the driver had raised the tinted privacy glass so he could be at his imaginary concert alone. Rhythm was something Sandino definitely hadn't inherited as he clapped his hands off beat.

🏈🏈🏈🏈🏈🏈🏈🏈

Three hours later, Sandino was laying on the bed with one of his old jumpoffs, Trina smoking weed, and drinking Coconut Ciroc. After reaching under the bed and grabbing a mirror with cocaine on it, Trina sniffed a line, then passed the mirror to Sandino. He looked at it. With all the bullshit going on in his life right now he needed to get high and the buzz from the weed wasn't strong enough.

After sniffing the powder, Sandino continued drinking and looked over at Trina who was wearing a white wife beater that made her plump booty beg for attention. The cute, ghetto fabulous girl was sprinkling weed into a Pink Berry Bluntville cigar when Sandino slapped her ass.

"Trina, who you been fuckin' while I was locked up?"

She lit the blunt and exhaled. "You got a wife and you still tryna keep tabs on this pussy? Nigga, get the fuck outta here," she said laughing. "Your ass don't own this."

"Wrong muthafuckin' answer, bitch," he said, slapping her across the face. "You think this shit is a game? Take them

119

fuckin' clothes off now!" he ordered.

Trina knew the drill. She'd been one of Sandino's side chicks ever since he got to Miami, so she knew better than to fight back. Instead, she placed the blunt in an ash tray by the bed and started slowly undressing.

"Hurry up. Don't play wit' me Trina!" he continued.

After taking off his clothes, Sandino reached over and grabbed a wad of Trina's off-black weave before pushing her back down on the bed. He then forcefully opened her legs and shoved his thick shaft inside her walls.

"Is that all you got nigga?" she moaned.

"You talkin' shit, huh, bitch?" he said, flipping Trina over on her stomach. He pushed her face so far into the pillow, she could hardly breathe.

"You hurtin' me!" Trina yelled even though her cries went unnoticed.

Beyond excited by this point, it wasn't long before Sandino pulled out of her pussy then rammed his dick in her ass with no lubrication. Although Trina was used to anal sex, Sandino's large dick was more than she could handle.

"Wait…it hurts Sandino!" Trina wailed.

Her pleads for him to stop still didn't phase Sandino as he thrust his manhood back and forth at a rapid speed. Taking her pussy felt good and got out tons of his bottled up aggression. When Sandino felt himself about to cum, he pulled out.

"Come suck my dick, bitch."

When she didn't move fast enough he grabbed her foot and drug her off the bed. "Get on your knees!" he demanded, punching her in the face.

"Sandino, what the hell is wrong with you?" Trina asked with tears in her eyes.

"This is what happens when you talk shit!"

When he grabbed her by the neck and crammed his dick inside her mouth, she instantly gagged, which caused Sandino to get even hornier. At that point, he pushed his tool even deeper.

"Please sto..," she tried to say.

"Shut the fuck up and suck!" he yelled, holding the back of her head.

Goose bumps covered her trembling body when she saw the rage in Sandino's face build up as he spoke. Trina sucked with force thinking she had to get it over with. A few minutes later, she heard his breathing intensifying and the grip on her head get tighter followed by a loud grunt when he released in her mouth. Trina knew she had to swallow. Spitting out his seed wasn't allowed.

As soon as he fell back onto the bed, Trina jerked her body away and moved to the other side of the room. Out of all the times they'd ever had sex, this time she never felt so humiliated.

"I see jail hasn't changed your crazy-ass," she finally said.

"Who the fuck said it would?" he responded.

Chapter Sixteen

Later that evening, Sandino sat in Trina's living room smoking on another blunt and waiting for her to fix him something to eat.

"Hurry the fuck up, Trina you slow as hell! You got a nigga out here starvin'?" he yelled.

A few minutes later, Trina walked out with a white paper plate that held a fried bologna sandwich and some seasoned curly fries. When Sandino looked at the food, he instantly frowned.

"What the hell is that? I'm not eatin' that bullshit," he said, grabbing the plate and throwing it up against the wall. "Do you think I'm still in fuckin' jail? I'm not about to eat no damn bologna. I ain't had that shit since I was six years old. Now, go in there and make me some real food, pasta or something," he demanded.

As soon as Trina rolled her eyes, Sandino jumped up in her face.

"Is there a problem? Do you need to get something off your chest?"

Trina wasn't in the mood for his temper. More importantly, she didn't feel like getting her ass kicked over some lunch meat.

"No, not at all. I'll find something else," she said walking around him.

After picking up the food and the plate off the floor, she made her way back into the kitchen.

"I'm sick of these dumb-ass broads," Sandino replied before sitting back down.

With the television up loudly, he directed his attention to Sports Center on ESPN. Surprisingly, they were showing a bad football highlight of the Miami Dolphins from a few weeks earlier. Sandino hated seeing his former team playing without him.

"You should've thrown the damn ball, Henne!" Sandino yelled.

As he watched the play unfold, he could see the protection break in the pocket and knew why the Dolphins quarterback got sacked.

"Coach Sparano's dumb-ass always runs the Forty-Two Blue every time. That single back formation wit' a screen pass to the runnin' back shit never works because everybody in the league knows he constantly runs that play." Sandino shook his head. "Henne never got sacked when I was in the game. Even wit' that stupid-ass play. They should've got rid of his ass instead of me!" he said, referring to his former head coach. "That's why they didn't make the play-offs!"

Sandino took his mind off the T.V. momentarily when Trina's cell phone rang. Expecting a call, Sandino hit the accept button as soon as he recognized the number.

"Yo," he answered.

"What up Sandino. This Dre. I got your message."

"Yo, what up? Damn, it took your ass long enough to hit me back."

Dre laughed. "I see you still impatient. It's only been about thirty minute's nigga, so calm down. Anyway, I saw your release on the news 'dis mornin'."

"Yeah that shit…"

Sandino was suddenly interrupted when Trina walked back into the room.

"Did my phone ring?" she asked with a fork in her hand. Her facial expression wondered why Sandino had her new Blackberry Torch up to his ear.

"Yeah, it did."

"So, who was it?" Trina questioned.

She hoped like hell Sandino wasn't having words with one of her other men. With her car note coming up, she didn't need any altercations.

"Bitch, obviously it wasn't for you if I'm on the phone," Sandino shot back. "Now, take your ass back in the kitchen." When Trina stomped away, Sandino yelled, "And don't come back out empty handed either!"

Placing the phone back to his ear, Sandino continued. "Anyway, like I was sayin' that shit was crazy. Them reporters were all up in my face as soon as I stepped out the damn gates."

"That's what happens when you a super star." Dre joked. "So, what's up?"

"I have a business proposition for you."

"Oh yeah, what is it? I hope it's about makin' some real paper, cause this broke shit ain't for me," Dre responded.

"Not over the phone nigga. Meet me over my bitches crib so we can talk about it."

Once Sandino gave him the address, Dre told him he was on his way, then hung up.

Sandino really liked Dre, who was his former cell mate in jail. After re-lighting the blunt and pulling on it a few times, Sandino's mind drifted back to the days he stood on the yard running his mouth about being in the NFL. Unfortunately, most of the inmates didn't believe or recognize him at first, so he constantly got asked tons of questions. Most inmates thought being locked up with a pro ball player was cool, while the others were straight haters.

Dre, who always stayed to himself on the yard, peeped a dude who was about to sneak up behind Sandino with a blade one day. Instead of turning the other cheek, he stepped to the guy and applied a serious chokehold, hoping the dude would pass out. It took five guards to pull Dre off, who ended up spending a week in the hole for his actions. Although they were always cool, Sandino respected him even more for saving his life after that.

I guess that nigga's like my guardian angel, Sandino thought.

Twenty minutes later, Sandino stood up from Trina's black, leather Lazyboy recliner when someone knocked on the door. As soon as he glanced through the peep hole and saw Dre, he quickly opened the door with a smile.

"What up my nigga?" Sandino greeted.

"Mannnn, what the hell are you doin' in 'dis neighborhood? This is where I caught my assault and battery charge eighteen months ago. I'm probably still a wanted man over here. I had to go to war wit' a few youngins who thought they could come in and steal my turf," Dre' said, giving Sandino some dap as he walked inside the apartment. He looked around to make sure it was safe to be there before he sat down and made himself comfortable.

"Man, you washed up in the drug game anyway. Ain't nobody checkin' for yo' old-ass over here," Sandino said.

"That may be true and I may be done wit' slingin' drugs, but I'll still fuck a nigga up if they step to me wrong. That shit will never change," Dre bragged.

Standing at 6'4, with a two-hundred and eighty pound physique, Dre looked very intimidating to most. The tattooed guns on his neck and the words *Thug Life*, going across his back didn't help either.

Sitting back down, Sandino didn't waste time passing Dre his fresh blunt. It wasn't long before the two men sat smoking weed and reminiscing about some of crazy shit they experienced in jail.

"So, what's 'dis business proposition you wanted to talk

to me about?" Dre asked.

"I was just about to bring that up. Do you remember when I used to talk about my wife all the time?"

Dre shook his head. "Yeah, I remember."

"Remember when I told you she left me and took my kids? Well, that's why I need your help. I need you to find her for me."

Dre chuckled. "Are you serious? So, you want me to be on some ole' Magnum PI type shit."

"Exactly."

"Man, you were in the joint for a minute. I just knew as soon as you got out she would be waitin' for your ass. Why don't you just call her and start beggin'. You know women like 'dat soft shit."

"It's not that easy."

"So, why do you wanna find her so bad? It's obvious that she doesn't wanna be found. Even if she wanted a divorce, is bein' by yourself 'dat bad nigga?"

At that moment Sandino lost his patience. "Look, that bitch took my kids and I want 'em back. Do you want the damn job or not? You said you broke, right?"

"Yeah, I am, but do you even have any money left? Didn't you get kicked out the league?"

"Don't worry about that nigga. All you need to be concerned wit' is that I'll pay you half the money now and if you find her I'll give you the rest."

Dre rubbed his thin mustache that he'd decided to let grow in. "Let me think about 'dis for a minute. You caught a nigga off guard wit' 'dis shit."

Dre pulled on the blunt thinking about the proposition when someone knocked on the door. Sandino walked over and peeped through the hole before opening it.

"What's up nigga?" Black yelled. He and Sandino gave each other some dap and a quick hug.

Neatly dressed in a pair of Hudson jeans, Prada loafers,

and a grey button down shirt, Black walked over to the couch and sat down. It wasn't long before Dre noticed Black passing Sandino some type of pills.

"Dre, this my right hand man, Black," Sandino introduced. "Black, this the nigga Dre I was tellin' you 'bout. The one who was locked up wit' me."

"Yeah, I heard about you. What up?" Black said, giving Dre some dap. He then grabbed the blunt sitting in the ash tray, took a huge pull and inhaled.

As Dre wondered what the pills were all about, Black continued to puff on the blunt until he suddenly snapped his fingers.

"Oh yeah, I almost forgot." Black reached in his pocket and pulled out a huge wad of money before tossing it to Sandino.

Sandino smiled then held the money up. "Yeah, I needed this. I'm not used to walkin' around wit' empty pockets." He looked at Dre. "You still think I'm broke nigga?"

As if she could smell currency in the air, Trina walked back in the room with a bowl in her hand. Quickly cutting her eye at the money, she placed the bowl on the table as Sandino examined the food. This time she'd prepared Ramen noodles with two pieces of grilled chicken breasts on top and some broccoli. Sandino really went off this time.

"You been in there all this time and this is what you came out wit'? Bitch maybe this is what the fuck you call a meal, but I don't eat shit like this. You told me you could cook. My wife could cook; she would never bring her man no shit like this!"

Trina was beyond sick of him by now. "Well, maybe you need to go find her and tell her to come cook for your ass!"

When Black and Dre started laughing, Sandino's blood began to boil. Not to be disrespected by any female, Sandino stood up and slapped Trina so hard, she instantly saw stars.

Jackie D.

"Say something else out of line bitch!" he warned.

Trina grabbed her throbbing face. "But that's the only thing I have left in the house to cook." She looked at the money Sandino had placed on the table. "If you give me some money, I'll go to the store."

"I'm not givin' your coke-head ass shit. Get the fuck out my face Trina!" Sandino yelled.

Trina walked away embarrassed by the fact that Sandino had played her in front of his friends.

Dre shook his head thinking, *Damn, I thought I had a short temper, but Sandino is off the chain. I see why his wife left his ass.*

"Yo, Black you seen that nigga Cruze?" Sandino asked then sat back down.

"Hell no, I ain't seen his punk-ass."

"That nigga is beyond foul. After all the shit I did for him he could've at least came to see me while I was locked up. I haven't heard from his ass since I dropped him off after that shit happened at the diner," Sandino replied.

"Yeah, that nigga probably still saltly about how shit went down, but fuck that nigga. He weak anyway," Black said.

"What about that bitch, Asia? Anybody seen her around?" Sandino continued.

Black shook his head. "Ain't seen her either."

"Well, I guess that was a dumb question because I know for a fact that bitch popped Keon. Do you know some bullshit-ass detectives came to question me about that shit while I was locked up? Talkin' 'bout I was the last one he called," Sandino stated. "I gave that bitches name up easily, cuz I wasn't about to go down for that shit."

"Her ass definitely skipped town by now," Black chimed in.

Sandino switched the subject. "Has Kareem tried to reach you again?"

"Nope. He only called that one time. When I asked if

129

they were still in Atlanta he said yeah. But when I him asked what area, he rushed me off the phone. It sounded like he really wanted to tell me though. I called the number back, but he wouldn't answer," Black informed.

"What's the number? Hopefully he'll pick up this time," Sandino said.

Black reached into his pocket and pulled out his phone. After blurting out the number, Sandino grabbed Trina's house phone and dialed Kareem's phone. He listened as the phone rang and then an automated voicemail came on.

Sandino slammed the phone down. "That bitch probably found out he called you!" He looked at Dre. "So, what are you gonna do nigga? I don't have all day. The reason why I even asked you to do this shit is because I remember you tellin' me you were from ATL. If you not up to the task, then I need to find somebody else."

After looking at the stack of money on the table, Dre finally decided to take Sandino up his the offer. Besides, he had nothing to lose. The trip to Atlanta was the key to him getting back on his feet. After paying all his lawyer fees, all his money was gone. He was dead broke

"Yeah, I'm down. All my people still in ATL, so 'dis shit might work out. Once I hit the streets, I should be able to get some information on her. What's her name? Do you have a picture?"

"Her name is Skye. Ain't too many black bitches walkin' around wit' that shit, so once you put that name out there, it shouldn't be hard," Sandino replied before turning to Black.

"Man, I looked for a picture of her when I went by the house to get the money, but I couldn't find one," Black informed.

As soon as Sandino was about to go off, it hit him that he'd burned any picture that had Skye in it one night after she left. "No picture. But I can tell you that she's about 5'6, light complexion, long hair and has the most beautiful green eyes."

"Cool, that'll help. Meanwhile keep callin' your son because he might just break and actually say where they are," Dre said.

"Sandino, I don't know why you never sent me," Black stated. "That's what I'm here for…to take care of shit."

"You know why I never sent you nigga," Sandino replied. *If you were gonna take that gun and assault charge, I needed your ass around.*

Dre looked at Sandino. "Why don't you go yourself?"

"Because the last thing I want is for people to see me ridin' around lookin' for her. Black people talk, so you never know, the shit just might get back to her, and that bitch might leave again. No…I want her to get comfortable. I wanna sneak up on her ass when she least expects it. Besides, I might take my agent's advice and go do that rehab shit. If I get my kids back, I at least want it to seem like I'm a good father."

"When do you wanna get 'dis done?" Dre questioned.

"As soon as possible. The sooner you find her…the better," Sandino replied.

Dre and Sandino talked a few more minutes about the plan before Sandino handed him ten thousand dollars. To make sure they were on the same page, Sandino reiterated that he would give Dre the rest of the money once he found Skye, which was fine since Dre planned to put his private eye skills to work.

"As soon as you find her, call me. I'll tell you what to do at that point," Sandino stated. "I might just have you bring my kids back, then throw in an extra fee to get rid of that bitch."

Dre turned to Sandino and looked at him with an odd expression. He was down for playing Private Eye, but killing someone, especially a woman was an entirely different playing field. *Well, maybe he'll change his mind about that part. In the meantime, it's time to find this bitch so I can get paid.*

Jackie D.

Chapter Seventeen

Skye was hard at work on her shift at one of downtown Atlanta's historic food spots called, *The Varsity*. Established in 1928, and home of the world's largest drive-ins, The Varsity was one of the most popular fast food restaurants in the entire city. Skye presented a fake smile every time she had to recite there famous slogan, "What'll ya have" to the customers as soon as they walked inside. It wasn't necessarily her dream job, or a top paying profession at some Fortune 500 company, but for now it would have to do. As long as she had money to pay her bills and put food on the table, she couldn't complain. Sandino had taken care of Skye all her life, so her first job was definitely a reality check.

The place was jammed packed as usual and since Skye was still in training and didn't know much about being a cashier, she had to be closely monitored by the head cashier named Flo who always seemed to have a funky-ass attitude. Skye did her best to get along with the mean, older woman because she really needed the job. Although Justice offered to help out, she refused to ever rely solely on another man.

It had only been two weeks since Skye started, but it felt like she'd been working there forever. Skye hated it. Her feet constantly had blisters and what she hated most of all was the fact that she went home every day with her red smock smelling like onion rings and chili.

Skye was so busy taking orders and busting tables since they were short staffed that day, she didn't even realize it was time for her break. She'd been there since seven that morning cutting up potatoes for their fresh cut fries, and it was now noon. She walked over to Flo.

"It's way past my break time. I'm going to take it now if you don't mind," Skye said.

Flo was at the counter cutting a piece of their famous apple pie for a customer when she turned and looked at Skye then around the restaurant.

"I'll let you know when it's time for your break. Do you not see all these people in here?" Flo asked, rolling her eyes and walking away.

Flo had worked there for almost twenty years and acted as if she owned the joint. An older heavy set white woman in her mid sixties and a bad blonde dye job, Skye couldn't re-member when the woman ever had anything nice to say. With a frown constantly pasted on her face, Skye wondered why she was so damn hateful all the time.

Instead of a having a confrontation, Skye held her com-posure and continued working. She took several orders for the famous chili cheese dogs and homemade ice cream during the busy lunch rush while trying to talk herself out of quitting at any moment. After nibbling on stuff all morning, luckily she wasn't hungry and didn't plan on using the break to eat. Skye could handle a lot of things, but after dealing with Sandino, disrespect wasn't one of them.

About an hour later and after the place had slowed down some Flo finally walked over to Skye.

"Now, you can take a break," she stated.

Skye grabbed her coat and quickly walked outside to get some fresh air before the wicked witch of the east changed her mind. She was determined not to let Flo ruin her day.

As Skye sat outside, she propped up her aching feet and removed one shoe before rubbing the bottom of her heel. She watched as the parking lot became full again, but was determined not to go back inside before her break was over.

When she finally got up, thirty minutes later, Skye noticed a man standing across the street looking at her. As the man continued to stare, she pulled her sunglasses down to get a closer look at him. After looking for only a few seconds, her heart felt like it was about to come out of her chest. Jumping up, Skye instantly ran back inside because the man looked just like Cruze. Same height, same skin tone…same premature dreads. She wasn't a hundred percent sure it was him, but didn't want to take any chances. Although she tried to take a deep breath, her anxiety skyrocketed when the man headed toward the restaurant's front door. Panicking, she took off running toward the back of the restaurant where her car was parked and jumped inside. Curious, Flo came running behind her.

"Where do you think you're going?" she yelled. "Your shift isn't over!"

"I have a family emergency, I have to go!" Skye replied.

Flo's pale skin turned red. "It's a packed house in there. You can't just leave knowing we're short staffed. If you don't get back in that restaurant, you're fired!"

"Well, fire me then bitch, I hated working here anyway!" Skye yelled, then pulled off. She was scared and furious at the same time.

"I can't believe it's because of Kareem that all this shit happened, I'm tried of running!" she yelled to herself. Skye gripped the steering wheel and shook it. She was so fucking mad at him.

Speeding down Spring Street and toward I-75, Skye almost hit several cars trying to get home so she could pick Payton up from Lydia's house and Jordan from school. Even though Lydia lived in the same building, Skye didn't even want Kareem to pick the baby up, especially if all of this was his fault.

With one hand on the steering wheel, she picked up her cell phone and called the shelter looking for Justice.

"BTC, how may I help you?" Mercedes answered while smacking her gum.

Skye took a deep breath before speaking. "Can I speak to Justice?"

"Who is this?" Mercedes asked with an attitude.

"You know who this is Mercedes, cut the shit!" Skye yelled.

"First of all, you better bring that shit down to a four, because right now you're at a nine and a half."

Skye wasn't in the mood to deal with her right now so she quickly changed her tone. "This is Janelle. Can I please speak to Justice?

"Bitch, Justice isn't here."

CLICK

"Oh my God. Mercedes is really testing me right now," Skye said. She dialed Justice's cell phone and waited for it to ring.

"Hello," he answered.

"Where are you?" Skye asked.

"I'm at the shelter, baby."

"I just called and Mercedes said you weren't there. That bitch is getting on my last nerve!" Skye belted. "I need you to meet me at my apartment. I think I just saw one of my husband's friends outside my job watching me."

"Are you serious? Are you okay? I know you're probably upset, but please drive careful."

"I'm fine. Just trying to get to my kids."

While on the phone, Justice thought he heard the bell on the shelter's door open, but quickly diverted his attention back to Skye.

"Okay hold tight, I'm on my way, baby," he said, hanging up the phone.

Justice grabbed his keys, walked out the office and then

locked the door. A few seconds later he bumped into Mercedes in the hall.

"Where do you think you're going?" she questioned him like a non-trusting wife.

"I'm headed out," he replied in a harsh tone. "Oh, and the next time my girl calls, don't ever lie and tell her I'm not here."

Mercedes tossed her wavy hair over her shoulder. "Oh, so she's your girl now, huh?" She didn't even give Justice a chance to respond, before tossing out the next question. "So, are you headed out to meet that bitch? Justice, you don't know anything about her, or where she even came from. You running behind her ass like a little puppy."

"Mercedes, mind your business. Nobody asked for your opinion."

"So, does she know that you were my man, first?"

Justice glared at her. "I wasn't your man and no, she doesn't need to know what happened between us that *one* time. And if you wanna keep working here, you better keep your fucking big mouth shut," he said, walking past Mercedes and heading out the door.

He quickly got into his car and tried to pull off, but didn't make it far when he realized something was wrong. When he got out to see what the problem was, rage consumed his body instantly.

"Fuck!" he yelled then walked around the entire car.

All four of his tires had been slashed.

"I know that bitch did this shit!" Justice said, running back into the shelter

When he reached Mercedes' office, she was sitting at her desk filing her nails and looking like an innocent child.

"Did you slash my fucking tires?"

She looked up. "What are you talking about?"

"Don't play stupid. Who else would do some juvenile shit like that, but you? Puerto Rican bitches love to walk around with knives so I know you did it! I'm so sick of your psycho-ass!"

Mercedes' face turned evil. "Psycho? Who the fuck are you calling psycho?"

"You!" Justice roared. "Do you know how much BMW tires cost?"

In an instant, Mercedes changed her tone. "I would never do that to you baby. Maybe you pissed somebody off. Are you sure it wasn't Janelle?"

Justice stood and looked at her for a minute. He wanted to fire her ass so bad, but knew he needed time to hire someone else. Besides, he didn't have anything to prove his accusations.

If she keeps this charade up her ass is outta here, he thought walking away and slamming his office door.

$$\text{❦❦❦❦❦❦❦❦}$$

Two hours later Justice finally arrived at Skye's apartment. When she opened the door he could tell she was pissed. Even though he'd called and told her what happened, Skye was still disappointed.

"Remind me never to call you in the event of a damn emergency," she stated in a sarcastic tone.

"I'm sorry, baby. It wasn't my fault."

"Do you think it was Mercedes who cut your tires? If so, she must really be in love with your ass. This whole obsession situation with you and that bitch is crazy as hell. Something isn't right about it either. Nobody acts like that over a friend."

"Trust me, that's all we've ever been." When Justice felt his phone vibrate, he reached on his side and saw a blocked number, but decided to answer it anyway.

"Hello, hello?" he yelled.

No answer.

Even though he hung up the phone and continued talking, Justice thought the caller was probably Mercedes.

"I mean she could've done it, but since I don't have any proof there's only so much I could do. I don't want to talk about that right now. Are you sure you're alright?" Justice walked over and hugged her. "Please forgive me for being late. I'll make it up to you. I promise."

Skye pulled away from his embrace and rubbed her sweaty palms on her jeans and sat on the couch. Her nerves were still fucked up. If that was Cruze outside her job then she knew it would only be a matter of time before Sandino would be on her doorstep.

Breaking down, Skye confided in Justice.

"This shit is crazy. I can't continue to live my life in fear."

"Are you sure it was your husband's friend?"

She shrugged her shoulders. "I don't know, maybe not. I'm probably just paranoid. Just like the day I thought he was chasing me in a gold Tahoe. I feel like I'm going crazy."

"Janelle, maybe I need to know who your husband is."

Still not comfortable about revealing her identity, she continued to cry. "I'm still not ready to talk about that right now."

He wondered what the big secret was, but decided not to press her any further.

"Okay, we have plenty of time to talk about that. In the meantime, I'm not going anywhere baby," he said, trying to kiss her.

She backed away. "I don't wanna get hurt, Justice."

"I promise, I won't hurt you. I love you and want to protect you. I have a big, nice house in Decatur. I want y'all to move in with me."

Skye seemed shocked. "Love me? But you've only known me for a few months."

"What does time have to do with anything? Trust me, I haven't felt this way about a woman in a long time," Justice responded. "Don't you have feelings for me?"

Before Skye could respond, Kareem walked into the room with an empty bowl in his hand.

"What is he doing here? You aren't even divorced yet, and you laying up with this nigga." Kareem walked into the kitchen and threw the bowl into the sink.

Justice looked at Kareem. He was sick of his ass, and could no longer hold his tongue. "Look Kareem, I don't know what your beef is with me, but I care about your mother and I'm not going anywhere. You can hate me all you want, but your mother doesn't deserve to be disrespected like that."

"Man whatever; I don't need you trying to tell me how to talk to my mother. You need to get the fuck out!"

Skye jumped up. "Have you lost your damn mind Karrem? Who the hell are you talking to?"

When Kareem walked to his room and slammed the door, Payton started screaming. Skye felt like she needed a drink. One thing was for sure, she was going to get a gun, because if Sandino ever decided to show up, she would be ready for his ass this time. She refused to run any longer. After Kareem's behavior, Skye turned to Justice.

"I guess that answers your question about us moving in."

Chapter Eighteen

"There's no way I can pay two thousand dollars for each for my sons to get out of jail. I just don't have that kind of money. I thought the purpose of you being my lawyer was to get their damn bail reduced!" Mercedes screamed into the phone.

"Ms. Guzman, the reason the bail is so high is because both of your sons were on probation at the time of their arrests. I'm sorry it's nothing I can do. I've been your lawyer for some time now, and I think the only way your boys are going to get their act together is to sit in jail for a while."

"Listen, I don't recall asking for your fucking advice right now. My sons don't belong in jail. They've been in there for over a week. I suggest you get on your damn job and do something to get them out now!" Mercedes yelled then slammed the phone down. She tried her best to hold it together. "That damn lawyer hasn't done anything but take my fucking money and my sons are still locked up," she said to herself.

The fact that Justice wasn't around for moral support and all his attention seemed to be going to Skye pissed her off. Mercedes had hoped things would be back to normal between the two of them once Skye moved out of the shelter, but instead she saw even less of him.

Since Justice seemed to be so pre-occupied and spending less time at the shelter, Mercedes knew something was going on. She feared that Justice was falling in love and it bothered her that he still had yet to ask about Joey and Manny.

Mercedes rolled her eyes. "I know he's probably still pissed off about that tire slashing incident, but his ass needs to get over that shit since he couldn't prove it was me."

She became even more irritated when her phone rang. She started not to answer it, but suddenly changed her mind thinking it might be Justice.

"Hello," she answered.

"You have a collect call from an inmate at, Marietta Youth Detention Center. Press one to accept this call, three to decline."

Mercedes took a deep breath and pressed the number one button. Her son, Joey immediately started asking questions as soon as the call was connected.

"Ma, why haven't you gotten us out yet?"

"Your lawyer is working on lowering your bail son. It's too high right now, and I don't have enough to get both of you out."

"How long is it gonna take?"

"I'm trying as hard as I can Joey. How is your brother holding up?"

"Not too good. I can hold my own in here, but you know he's not built like that. How did Kareem get out? Didn't we have the same charge?"

"Yes, but you all have a probation violation charge, too."

"Can't Justice help you with our bail?" he drilled.

"I don't know. I'll see...just hold tight."

After talking for a few more minutes, the operator interrupted their conversation. "You have one minute left on this call."

"Ma, please. You gotta hurry up and get us outta here." The hard sounding Joey had turned into a frail little boy.

Suddenly, a tear rolled down Mercedes' face. She loved

her sons more than anything.

"I will Joey. I prom…"

The call was disconnected.

Mercedes hung up the phone and dropped her head on the desk. It seemed as if her head had only been down a second when Stephanie, one of the women at the shelter barged in her office.

"Mercedes we're out of sanitary napkins," she blurted out.

Mercedes stared angrily at the petite woman. "First of all, you must've lost your mind by barging into my office. Secondly, I know you're not worrying me about some fucking Kotex. I got bigger problems right now."

Even though Mercedes was the only staff member with keys to the supply cabinet that contained personal hygiene products and all the basic toiletries, she could care less when the women needed anything half the time. With her mind constantly consumed about Justice most days, her response was always the same, "I'll get that shit in a minute."

"Listen, you're gonna have to wait Stephanie, I'm busy," Mercedes snapped.

"But you're not doing shit. Besides, I can't wait. I need them really bad, my flow is heavy," Stephanie continued.

"Does it look like I give a fuck right now? You better stuff some tissue in your panties until I finish what I'm doing. Don't ever walk in my damn office without knocking. I'm not on your time!"

Stephanie looked at Mercedes and shook her head. "You're a real bitch Mercedes, especially when Justice isn't around. I can't wait to tell him how you've been treating all the women around here."

"Get the fuck out my office!" Mercedes yelled. She grabbed a pen off her desk and threw it as Stephanie turned around and slammed the door. "I'ma make sure she's the next bitch to leave here."

Infuriated once again that Justice wasn't around to deal with the nagging women, Mercedes decided to sneak into his office and go though Skye's file. Willing to bet her entire paycheck that he was over Skye's house, Mercedes needed the file to locate her new address. The state required that the shelter keep up with all occupants for the first two years, so finding out where Skye laid her head at night was the easy part. Locating the key to the file cabinet where Justice kept all the information locked up was another issue. She had access to his office, but all occupant folders were off limits.

Heading down the hall, Mercedes constantly looked around to make sure no one was watching as she made her way to his office. When the coast was clear she unlocked the door and slipped inside.

Not wasting any time, Mercedes quickly used the rubber band that was around her wrist to place her hair in a ponytail then opened every drawer inside Justice's desk. Seeing Justice open the cabinet numerous times, she knew what the small key looked like, but couldn't find it. Looking under his rolodex, his dice paperweight and even inside his candy dish, Mercedes was about to give up when suddenly it hit her.

Every time Justice was about to go to the cabinet, she would always hear the CD drive on his computer pop open. Not thinking anything of it until now, Mercedes wiggled the mouse to his computer to activate the power. Knowing Justice always kept this computer in sleep mode, Mercedes quickly hit the button to eject the CD drive, then smiled once she saw the small, gold key tapped inside.

"Bingo," she said with a conniving smile.

After retrieving the key, Mercedes walked over to the cabinet and opened it with ease before quickly thumbing through the folders. Once she landed on the one that said, *Janelle Coleman*, her smile became even wider.

Excited by this point, Mercedes read through Justice's notes during their sessions, then finally made her way to the section that stated…current location.

"I know exactly where this is," she said, writing down the address.

When she finished, Mercedes placed the file back in the same location then proceeded to close the door, However, when she spotted Stephanie's folder, Mercedes decided to get her ass back for being such a pain. She knew Stephanie was a former drug addict, who allowed her boyfriend to abuse her along with her four kids. She also knew that Stephanie was trying to get her kids back from several foster homes. Although Stephanie was now sober and clean, Mercedes wrote some false shit about her being caught using drugs at the shelter in the back of her records, so the state could see it whenever they reviewed her file. Justice did such a half-ass job when the women were released sometimes, he probably wouldn't notice the false information.

"That should teach your ass not to call me a bitch," Mercedes said as she put the file back and closed the cabinet door.

After placing the key back, Mercedes made sure everything was in order before leaving Justice's office. She then went to the supply cabinet in the hallway, and unlocked it, before pulling out a box of sanitary napkins. When she passed Stephanie's room, Mercedes threw the box at her.

"There you go bloody Mary, "she said laughing out loud.

"You need help," Stephanie responded.

Like a woman on a mission, Mercedes went back to her office, grabbed her purse and keys, then headed to her car. Her man was more than likely over another woman's house, and he needed to know that was totally unacceptable.

ㅤ*ﾟﾟﾟﾟﾟﾟﾟ*

While driving, Mercedes wondered why all the relationships in her life never worked out. It was a known fact that she'd given each man her all, but after they got what they wanted from her, they always left. However, this time she wasn't letting it go down like that. Deep down in her heart, Mercedes knew she and Justice were meant to be.

If that bitch, Janelle, thinks she's gonna set up house with my man like they're one big happy family, she better think again. His place is with me and my boys, that's his fucking family, she thought.

Several minutes later, Mercedes pulled into Skye's neighborhood. When she did a thorough scan of the parking lot, it didn't take long for her to locate Justice's car. She was furious.

Banging the steering wheel, she yelled, "That bitch!"

After parking her car a few rows from his, Mercedes quickly jumped out. Ducking down, she ran over to Justice's car and pulled out a spare key that she'd made a long time ago without him knowing. After getting inside, she looked around and saw a sweatshirt in the back seat. Picking it up, she put it up to her nose and inhaled.

"I love the way my man smells," she said smiling. She laid back in the seat and rubbed the leather. "I'm going to look good driving this shit to pick up my boys."

Looking around the car, Mercedes instantly sat up when she noticed a silver hoop earring on the floor of the passenger's side. She was furious all over again.

"I can't believe he had that bitch is this car!"

Reaching in her jacket pocket, Mercedes pulled out her phone and called Justice's number with her long nails within seconds.

"Hello," he said.

The minute she heard his voice, she started screaming. "Justice something bad has happened. There's been a fire at the shelter!"

"Oh my God, are you serious? Did anybody get hurt? Where are you?" Justice frantically asked.

"Everybody is fine. I'm here at the shelter with the fire chief. Almost everything was destroyed. You need to get over here right away! It's bad…it's really bad." Mercedes had to cover her mouth to keep from laughing.

"Stay right there, I'm on my way!" Justice yelled before hanging up.

With a wicked grin on her face, Mercedes quickly took off her long sleeved t-shirt and bra then jumped in the back seat and bent down on the floor. She watched as Justice ran out of Skye's apartment and toward the car. Because his windows were tinted, he had no way of knowing she was inside.

When he jumped in the car and put the key in the ignition, Mercedes popped her head up scaring Justice half to death.

"Hey daddy, I've missed you!"

Justice was shocked and furious at the same time. "How the hell did you get in my damn car?"

She smiled and daggled the spare key in his face. "This is how."

Justice tried to snatch the key, but Mercedes pulled her hand back and laughed.

"Why the hell are you playing these silly little games and what are you doing here? Where the hell are your clothes?" he questioned.

"I should be asking you the same fucking thing! You should be at work, not over here with this bitch!"

"How did you find out where Janelle lived?" Justice asked. He suddenly remembered his files. "Did you go into my file cabinet, Mercedes?"

"Yes, I had to get her address so I could come over here and talk some sense into you."

"Mercedes, you've gone too fucking far this time."

At that point, she reached over the seat and wrapped her arms around his neck.

"Justice, you don't understand. I love you. Please don't

mess up what we have for her." She then grabbed his hand and fondled her breast. "Don't you miss this baby?"

Annoyed, Justice immediately pulled his hand back. "What *we* have? Mercedes I'm going to tell you this one last time. What we *did* was a mistake. We'll never be together! Now leave me the fuck alone and get out my damn car!"

"No, I'm not getting out until we discuss working on our relationship," Mercedes pouted.

Fed up, Justice got out the car, walked around to the back door and pulled her out. Instead of trying to cover her bare chest, Mercedes started screaming making a huge scene as several onlookers stared in disbelief. Justice looked over in the direction of Skye's apartment to make sure she hadn't heard the commotion.

"I don't believe this shit. You're fucking crazy, don't come back to work, you're fired!" he yelled.

Getting up off the ground, Mercedes yelled back, "So, you're gonna fire me after all we've been through?"

Justice reached in his car and grabbed her belongings then threw them at her. "Yes, I am."

"You can't do this!" Mercedes screamed.

Not wanting to entertain her antics any longer, Justice started walking back to Skye's apartment.

"Justice…Justice…does Ms. Janelle know that you're married?"

He immediately stopped walking and turned around. "No, and if she ever finds out, trust me…you'll be sorry.

Chapter Ninteen

Driving for six straight hours, Dre loved the way the new Chevrolet Camaro V8, 400 horsepower engine handled the road.

"Hopefully after this job I can get me one of these," he said, rubbing the rental car's steering wheel like a fine piece of china.

He wondered what was in store for him now that he was out of jail and no longer a drug dealer. He didn't understand where his life went wrong. Despite having a good upbringing he always found himself in trouble.

"Maybe I'll go legit and invest in some type of business, or get married and have a couple of kids," Dre mumbled to himself.

Knowing he was two days behind schedule since Trina refused to rent the car at first, Dre stepped on the gas so he could get to Atlanta at a decent time. He turned up the radio when his favorite Maxwell song, *Lifetime* came on, and instantly sang along with the lyrics.

"*I was reborn when I was broken, I wouldn't believe, I wouldn't believe.*"

When he started thinking about his old girl, a burn of arousal ignited in his blood. As mean and evil as Dre could be at times, she was the only woman that he ever dated who could soften him up. He'd never let a woman get close to him, but somehow she'd managed to break through the huge tough barrier to his heart.

When they were dating, he liked the fact that she wasn't a push over like the rest of the women in his past. She would go toe to toe with his ass and never backed down. That shit turned Dre on. He wanted to make her his wife and give her the world. So when he got an opportunity to go set up shop in Miami and make some real money, he left her and Atlanta behind. Unfortunately, she was still holding it against him. Getting locked up wasn't in Dre's plan, but sometimes it came with the territory.

As soon as thoughts about the good times they shared together entered his mind, Dre pulled out the cell phone that Sandino gave him and decided to give her a call. He hoped she hadn't changed her phone number since his last attempt. He'd stopped trying to call a while back because she refused to answer or even come see him while he was locked up.

Anxious to hear her voice, he listened as the phone rang and surprisingly this time she answered.

"Hello," she said in the sexy tone he remembered so well.

His face displayed a huge grin. "Oh, my goodness. What up, Baby Girl?"

His voice rippled with excitement, but there was dead silence on the line for about two seconds. She was surprised to hear from him.

"Don't hey, baby girl me, Dre." Her sexy tone now sounded bitter and angry.

"Please don't act like 'dat, baby. You know I love me some you."

She sighed with frustration. "Yeah right. Obviously you love them streets that you left me for even more."

Hearing her say that made him feel like shit. Going away and leaving her was the last thing he ever wanted to do.

"I was tryin' to make a better life for us. But don't

worry, that was the old Dre."

"You out?" she asked when she heard the radio playing in the background.

"Yes, I'm out and actually headed your way. Can I come see you?"

"You think you can just call and pick up where we left off?"

"No, I'd be a fool to think 'dat, but I still wanna see you. I've missed you."

Once again there was dead silence.

"Look, I'm not in the mood for you and all your bullshit right now," she replied. "Besides, you might get your feelings hurt if you come see me."

"Why?" Dre questioned.

"Because I'm involved with someone else."

"So…I'm not trippin' off 'dat shit." Dre quickly shot back. "Now, are you gonna let me come over when I get there or what?" He looked at the clock on the dashboard. "It's ten minutes after seven. I should be there around ten."

"I'll be asleep by then."

"Asleep? Stop lyin'. You ain't never went to bed that early. I know you still a night owl."

She sucked her teeth. "You ain't shit Dre, but you always did have some good dick and I could use some of it right now. I'll text you my address."

Click.

Smiling so hard his cheeks hurt, Dre was super excited about getting paid and getting his girl back. Her remark about being involved with someone else didn't sit right with him. He still loved her and wasn't going to let another man take his place.

"I'll hurt the nigga if he gets in my damn way," he said to himself.

🏈🏈🏈🏈🏈🏈🏈🏈

After walking up to his girl's door, Dre let out a huge sigh as if he was going out on his first date. He was actually nervous about seeing her and wiped his sweaty palms on his shirt trying to get himself together. It had been over a year since he'd seen her so the butterflies in his stomach would not go away. As tired as he was from the long nine hour drive, the excitement from seeing his girl gave him an instant rush.

He'd stopped by the store and picked up some flowers a bottle of wine and even managed to find a small jewelry store and picked out a cute silver necklace with a diamond heart. He wanted to show her just how much he'd missed her.

Taking a deep breath, Dre knocked on the door as the butterflies continued to swarm around his stomach. Hoping she hadn't changed her mind, he patiently waited for her to come to the door.

Moments later, Mercedes slowly opened the door and surprisingly jumped into his arms. Dropping all the goodies he had on her living room floor, Dre hugged her warm body. She was wearing a short, black t-shirt with the word, *Hottie* on the front along with some black lace panties. She was still sexy as hell, which immediately turned him on.

Even though Dre was surprised by her actions, he brushed it off not caring about the past, and focused on his rock hard dick. He hadn't had sex in eighteen months and planned to blow her back out.

"Hey, Baby Girl," he whispered in her ear. "You still gorgeous."

The two kissed passionately as he carried her in the direction that looked like it lead to the bedroom. While going down the long narrow hallway he looked around and couldn't help but notice how dirty her place was. It was shit everywhere.

Damn, I don't remember her bein' 'dis nasty, he thought.

Trying to block it out of his mind, they continued kissing as Dre kicked the bedroom door open, then laid Mercedes on the bed and removed her panties. He rubbed his hands across her smooth skin and sniffed her body. Her natural body scent was more seductive than any perfume. One of the things he missed almost as much as pussy while locked up was the smell of a woman. Dre couldn't wait to taste her as he made his way down to her wetness and softly sucked her outer lips, savoring every moment.

"You must've forgotten how to eat pussy with all that soft licking shit. Eat my pussy like you missed it!" Mercedes demanded with authority.

Like a trained student, Dre dove in head first sucking and licking with aggression. When he did circular motions with his tongue across her clit, Mercedes moaned in pleasure letting him know she was now satisfied. After thrusting his tongue in and out and licking her juices, Dre began to stroke his dick with his free hand.

When he could no longer control himself he told her, "Turn around baby."

He knew Mercedes loved to be fucked doggie style as she smiled, turned around and got on all fours. With her hands, she reached behind and spread her ass cheeks wide open.

"You better act like you missed this. You know I like it rough!"

Dre slapped her firm ass before entering her pussy from behind giving her all ten inches. She arched her back as he went deeper with his strokes. She knew how to tighten her pussy on his dick driving him crazy.

"Damn Baby Girl, I missed 'dis pussy," Dre mumbled.

She felt so good, he was close to exploding, but he held it as long as he could. He knew she would go the hell off if he came too soon. When he heard her yell out that she was cumming, that was his green light as he too began to shake uncontrollably.

"I want 'dis pussy to be all mine," Dre moaned as he released.

And not give Justice anymore of this...I don't think so, Mercedes thought.

They both collapsed taking a short intermission before the next sex session began.

❧❧❧❧❧❧❧❧

The next morning, Dre woke up to the smell of bacon. He laid in bed and smiled thinking; *my baby must be hungry after the wild night of sex we had.* He'd almost forgotten just how kinky she was. His dick got hard just thinking about how warm and cozy her pussy was.

"I could use some of her lovin' right now," Dre said, rubbing his manhood.

He couldn't believe that Mercedes had finally answered his call and allowed him to come over after all this time. He also couldn't help but wonder what the change of heart was all about.

Thinking back to when they first met, Dre could admit that he had love for Mercedes ever since he laid eyes on her years ago. He was at a party hosted by her boyfriend, Quentin a well known dealer in Atlanta who was also his connect. That particular night, Dre remembered Mercedes walking into the living room and asking him where valet should park the extra cars. He was shocked when Quentin literally cursed her out in front of everyone, called her stupid, then excused himself from the party. Dre couldn't believe the way he spoke to her, and hoped his boy knew how lucky he was to have such a beautiful woman in his life.

An hour later, a tipsy Dre walked around their huge house in search of the bathroom. However, instead of finding it, he found a badly beaten and hysterical Mercedes instead.

He felt bad as she cried like a newborn baby in the doorway of their kitchen. Dre wished like hell he could tell her everything would be alright, but he wasn't into giving anyone false hopes. So, he did the only thing he could think of to somewhat ensure her safety.

"Here, take my keys and go hide in my truck, it's the black Yukon Denali. I got a blanket in the back seat. Get underneath it. I'll knock on the window three times to let you know it's me. Then we can get you to safety."

A little hesitant at first, Mercedes eventually took the keys, secretly made her way to the back door then limped toward his truck as Dre watched to make sure Quentin wasn't coming. Dre returned to the party as if nothing happened, but ultimately slipped out the backdoor himself a few minutes later.

After safely making it away from her house, he drove Mercedes to his place where it took days to nurse her back to health. Dre was highly respected and had a lot of clout in the streets. He was known for shooting nigga's first and asking questions later. So when Quentin came looking for her a few days later, the two had a confrontation. Dre ultimately threatened to harm his mother if he didn't leave Mercedes alone, and just like the punk he was…Quentin backed off. It wasn't long before Dre and Mercedes became a couple. He even took her to North Carolina to get her sons, whom she hadn't seen in months due to Quentin's controlling ways. They were happy for awhile. Unfortunately his decision to go to Miami got in the way of their once blissful relationship.

Dre heard his phone ringing. After grabbing and seeing the 305 area code, he knew it was probably Sandino.

"Hello," he answered.

"What's up Dre? Just checkin' to see if you made it safely."

"Yeah, I'm here, just woke up actually."

"Well, get your ass up and hit them streets. You got shit to handle, time is money," Sandino said.

"I'm on it man. I'll hit you up as soon as I have some info."

"Alright my nigga," Sandino replied then ended the call.

Dre rolled over in bed and rubbed the sheets. He definitely planned to go eat and bring Mercedes back to bed so they could fuck all day. He had a lot of catching up to do, so finding Sandino's wife would have to go on the back burner for now.

After getting out of bed, he put on his underwear and looked around her room. It was a mess just like the rest of the apartment.

"She needs to clean 'dis shit up." He wondered why she was no longer living in the nice apartment he'd set her up in before he left for Florida. "This place is a fuckin' dump."

When Dre walked into the dining room, he was surprised to see Mercedes sitting at the table eating and reading a magazine. She completely ignored the other dirty cups and plates sitting on the table in front of her.

He walked over and tried to plant a huge kiss on her lips, but she moved her head away.

"So, it's like 'dat? Where my food at? You didn't fix me a plate?" he inquired.

She grabbed a piece of bacon and put it in her mouth.

"Hold up...that looks like pork bacon. Guess you forget I only eat turkey bacon," he continued.

"First of all, I didn't cook you shit and secondly I don't give a damn what you eat. It's time for you to get the fuck out of here anyway. And make sure you take this cheap, fake-ass necklace with you," she said, rolling her eyes.

Mercedes tossed the necklace on the floor and continued to flip through the magazine.

Dre looked completely confused. "What the hell did I miss? Why are you actin' like 'dis? I thought we had a good time last night?"

"We did have a good time. Your dick was good as usual. It was just what I needed right now."

"Baby Girl, I know you still mad at me for leavin', but it wasn't the place for you or the boys. You need to let 'dat shit go so we can work 'dis out. If you would'a answered my calls you would know 'dis by now. I've been tryin' to explain 'dis shit to you for over a year," Dre pleaded. He suddenly remembered that he hadn't even seen her sons. "Where are the boys anyway?" he asked.

Mercedes looked up from the magazine with an annoyed expression. "They're in jail on drug charges and the reason I didn't except your fucking calls was because I told you that I found someone else to take your place!"

Dre's eyes enlarged. He was shocked to find out about Joey and Manny, but also surprised that Mercedes wasn't joking about her moving on. "Oh, really."

"Yes. What…did you expect me to wait for you? Please. That shit would've never happened."

"So, who is it?"

"Does it even matter Dre?

"Yes it does. Who the fuck is it?

"Your brother!" Mercedes yelled out.

Chapter Twenty

Dre stood in shock after hearing Mercedes last words.

He was trying to get his self together and understand what was going on. It took every ounce of his strength not to slap the shit out of her.

"Mercedes, what the fuck you mean, my brother?"

"You heard me. Since you ran off and left me I moved the fuck on with my life."

He sat down. *Even though me and Mercedes weren't headed down the aisle, she was the closest thing to being my wife. That shit is foul that my brother moved in on my territory.*

"Dre, do you know that when you left town, I ran back into Quentin at South Dekalb Mall, and he literally whooped my ass in the food court. I was in the hospital for two weeks. Luckily Justice was there for me. He hid me and the boys until they locked Quentin up.

"I'm sorry, Baby Girl. I had no idea," Dre said.

Mercedes shrugged her shoulders like she didn't care. "Justice and I are in love. I was pregnant with his baby but suffered a miscarriage." She took a deep breath. "We're planning to get married really soon, so consider us officially over," Mercedes said in a firm and convincing tone. Dre never knew she was lying.

Seconds later, she walked into her bedroom and closed the door.

Her statement took Dre totally off guard. It was the last thing he expected her to tell him. He also couldn't believe that Mercedes was throwing the fact that she was with Justice up in his face. Needing to get to the bottom of this, he grabbed the phone and immediately called his brother.

When Justice answered the phone he was glad to hear from Dre, especially since Justice didn't know Dre was out of jail. His nonchalant behavior made Dre wonder if Mercedes was telling the truth or if she was just trying to get back at him for leaving her. The brothers talked for a few minutes before Dre suggested they meet up. Agreeing, Justice gave Dre the address and told him to come by his job. He also gave him the code to the front door, so Dre wouldn't have to wait outside. Now that Mercedes was no longer working there, Justice didn't have time to keep running to the door, and didn't allow his occupants to answer it under any circumstances.

In a hurry, Dre went to go grab his clothes out of Mercedes' bedroom. He was just about to knock when the door swung wide open. He watched as she came out wearing a long wedding dress and a veil.

"Don't I make a beautiful bride?" Mercedes asked, twirling her body around and looking at herself in the mirror.

Dre couldn't believe she was rubbing the betrayal in his face like it was cool. "So, you really plannin' on marryin' my damn brother Mercedes?"

"Yes, I told you, we're in love."

He shook his head in disgust. "We'll see bout that."

After putting back on his clothes and grabbing the car keys, Dre walked to the front door. Mercedes followed him.

"I've been so busy lately with all the planning for our wedding. Your good dick was exactly what I needed to relieve my stress," she said, rubbing his chest.

"So that's it. We're over?" Dre asked then unlocked the door.

"Yeah, but feel free to stop by and hit me off anytime.

Justice and I have an open relationship," Mercedes said just as Dre stormed out.

She didn't waste anytime slamming the door in his face.

🏈🏈🏈🏈🏈🏈🏈🏈

As Dre headed toward Stone Mountain, visions of his brother and the love of his life in bed together enraged him. If Mercedes was telling the truth about their upcoming marriage, it was definitely going to be hard pill to swallow.

When Dre pulled up at the shelter a few minutes later, he got out of his car and looked around. *What the fuck is he doin' out here,* he thought looking at the house.

After glancing around the premises, Dre walked up to the door, punched in the code Justice gave him and walked inside. As he made his way through the shelter, he wondered what type of place it was. He knew his brother was always trying to open some type of nonprofit organization and thought maybe the shit had finally happened for him.

"The place needs some work though," Dre said to himself.

Seconds later, Stephanie walked up to him and eyed him up and down.

"Who are you?" she asked.

"I'm Deuce's brother," Dre responded.

"Deuce? Ain't nobody around here named Deuce. How did you get in here? I'm calling the police. Don't…"

Before she could continue, Justice suddenly appeared in the hallway.

His smile was as wide as Texas. "Calm down, Stephanie. He's my brother," Justice said. He walked up and gave Dre a strong, manly hug.

Dre was standoffish and didn't hug him back. He knew he shouldn't let a bitch come between his blood, but he couldn't believe his brother would do him like that and not even bother to mention it to him when he called from jail once a month.

Stephanie quietly walked away when she realized everything was okay.

"Damn bro. You look like you've been pumping a ton of iron in there." Justice said as he looked at Dre. "Come on…follow me into my office."

Once the two walked inside, Justice closed the door behind them.

"So, why didn't you tell me that you were getting out? How did you get here?" Justice questioned.

"All of that is a long story bro."

Justice stared at his baby brother. "That answer sounds shady. Are you into some shit already?"

Dre shook his head. "No…not at all."

"I still can't believe how much weight you've gained. Remember how skinny you used to be back in the day?" Justice teased.

"Yeah, all 'dat runnin' and stayin' up all night on 'dem street corners had a nigga stressed. All that shit is behind me now though."

"We'll see, lil' bro," Justice replied with doubt.

"So, what kind of place is 'dis? Some type of drug rehab?" Dre changed the subject before he went the hell off on his still negative-ass brother.

"No, it's a battered women's shelter. I decided to open it in honor of our mother."

"That's what's up, Deuce. I gotta give it to you, your ass is always into somethin'. You know how to make a damn dollar," Dre admitted. "I need to get into some legit shit like 'dis."

Justice shook his head. "Don't call me that. I don't really go by that anymore."

"Since when? Nigga, I been callin' you Deuce forever. What's the big deal now? What…you don't gamble anymore? When's the last time you lost all your dough in Vegas, nigga?"

Dre eyed his brother's crisp Armani sweater. "I see you still dressin' nice."

Dre smiled, but Justice didn't find anything amusing.

"I don't do any of that shit anymore. I took my money and opened this shelter. Speaking of the shelter, Mercedes was one of the first women to stay here. After getting the counseling she needed, she decided to take a full time position."

Dre figured that was probably how their affair got started. He wondered how long his brother was going to sit there before he told him he'd fucked his ex girl.

Dre continued to listen about the shelter when suddenly a light bulb went off in his head, *maybe Justice can help me find Sandino's wife,* he thought.

"So, do you have information on all the women who check into battered shelters in the state of Georgia?" Dre questioned.

"Yes. Actually the database I can log onto covers the entire country."

"Really. So, can anybody get into 'dat database?'"

"No, not at all. Not if you don't have a password. All the files are confidential."

"So, let me ask you 'dis…has a woman named Skye Washington been here by any chance? She has long hair, green eyes and…"

Justice quickly interrupted. "No, that name doesn't sound familiar. Why are asking?"

Dre shrugged his shoulders. "Just curious."

Justice looked at his brother a little suspicious, but decided to leave it alone.

After talking for a few more minutes Justice asked Dre to lunch, but he declined the offer.

"No, I got some shit to handle," he said, realizing he had to get to work on trying to find Sandino's wife.

"What you gotta do, go sell some drugs and get into trouble again?"

Dre smirked at his brother. "Thanks for the trust and positive thoughts, but I no longer sell drugs."

"That's great news. I just have your best interest at heart, always have. I want you to learn from your mistakes," Justice scolded.

Dre got pissed off and stood up.

"You got the nerve to try and give me some damn advice. Wit' all the shit you did in your past. You didn't have a problem wit' me sellin' drugs when I was supplyin' your ass wit' 'dat money for all your gamblin' and get rich quick schemes that never worked. You're such a fuckin' hypocrite. You not even man enough to tell me you been sleepin' wit' Mercedes!"

Justice lowered his head. "That was a mistake. It only happened one time and I've felt like shit ever since."

"Well, that's not what Mercedes said. I just left her house and she said y'all were in love and gettin' married. She even showed me her weddin' dress."

Justice couldn't help but laugh. "Get the fuck outta here, she told you what? Man that broad is crazy. I'm not with her. I had to fire her ass cause after that one night she's been bugging out ever since. You really need to stay away from her... that bitch needs to be evaluated."

Dre couldn't believe what he was hearing. "I was tryin' to figure out how you were gonna marry her when you're not even divorced yet. Does Felicia know you had an affair?"

Justice stopped smiling. He felt uncomfortable every time that name was mentioned. "Felicia and I are separated. She left me right after you got locked up."

"For what?"

"We just couldn't see eye to eye when it came to our finances," Justice admitted.

Dre smiled. "So, basically she left your ass because you kept losin' all your money, right?"

Justice smiled back. "Yeah."

"So, have you filed for divorce?" Dre inquired.

"Not yet. I'm working on that though."

"Shit, you crazy as hell because Felicia's ass was paid. How could you let a plastic surgeon leave you?"

Justice shook his head. *I miss that money too*, he thought.

"I just don't understand why Mercedes would lie like 'dat knowin' I would find out the truth," Dre said.

Justice felt his cell phone vibrate in his pocket. When he recognized Mercedes number he told his brother, "Here go the crazy broad calling now. Hopefully you'll believe me after this call," he said, putting the phone on speaker. "Hello."

"Justice, why the hell are you avoiding my calls?" Mercedes asked.

"Mercedes how many times do I have to tell you to leave me alone? Stop stalking me. When are you gonna understand that I don't want you."

"You don't mean that. You're just confused right now, that bitch has gotten in your head. We will be together!"

"No, the hell we won't, Mercedes."

"Yes, we will!"

As Dre listened, he was convinced that Mercedes had lost it. Justice ended the call by just hanging up in her face.

"You see what the fuck I have to deal with every day? That's why I had to fire her ass."

Dre laughed. He loved Mercedes, but obviously her mental state had altered a little bit since he'd been locked up.

"This shit ain't funny. That's your girl, you should've taken her crazy-ass with you and maybe none of this would've happened," Justice joked. "But I'm sorry for stepping over the line. That shit will never happen again."

"Apology accepted, bros before hoes," Dre responded.

Dre got up, gave his brother some dap, then said he'd call him later. After walking out of the office, his eyes lit up like sunshine when he accidentally bumped into the most beautiful woman he'd ever seen.

"I'm so sorry," he uttered.

Skye smiled. "It's okay. I'll live."

"What's your name?" Dre asked as he looked her up and down.

Skye wondered who he was. "Uh, you don't need to know all that," she shot back.

"Well, can I at least take you to dinner?"

"No, I don't think that would be a good idea."

"Why not?" Dre hated to be so persistent, but he didn't want a gorgeous woman like that to get away.

"Because she's my girl," Justice responded as he came out of his office. He walked straight over to Skye and planted a big kiss on her lips.

"Janelle baby, I want you to meet my brother, Dre," Justice introduced.

Skye extended her hand. "Nice to meet you."

Dre displayed an embarrassing grin. "My bad, Deuce. I had no idea."

Justice gave his brother a crazy look after hearing the nickname. "No problem."

"Well, let me get out of here. I'll call you later, bro," Dre said then made his way toward the door.

Damn she was bad. I wouldn't want Mercedes crazy-ass either if I had her, he thought just before jumping into his car.

Chapter Twenty~One

Sandino and Black sat in the small VIP section with the intoxicating mix of people partying at the popular hot spot, Club Lux in Miami Beach. Sandino's boy Chris who played for his former team was celebrating his new contract, so the place was jammed packed. At the advice of his agent and lawyer, Sandino had been laying low since he got out of jail. He was starting to feel down that no teams had expressed interest in him, so after receiving the call from Chris to come hang out, he didn't hesitate getting out of the house.

Shooing away several thirsty, groupie bitches who wanted free drinks, Sandino reached over and grabbed the bottle of Moet Rose' off the table just as the DJ played the old song *Knuck If You Buck* by Crime Mob. The crowd immediately started yelling. Some of the people in the cramped VIP section next to Sandino's got a little too excited and started jumping and stumbling into his side. Sandino became pissed when one of them stepped on his five-hundred dollar Louis Vuitton loafers.

"Watch where the fuck yo' broke-ass steppin', nigga," Sandino said pushing the guy.

"Who the fuck you calling broke?" the ice grilled dude fired back. He grabbed a wad of money out his pocket and flashed it. "You don't even play in the league no more nigga!"

"Get your fake ballin' ass back on your side before I

fuck you and your lil crew up!" Sandino yelled over the music.

Feeling brave, the dude all of a sudden threw a blow that landed right on Sandino's face. All hell broke loose after that. Chairs and bottles were being thrown as people screamed and scattered for safety. Black and Sandino were out numbered…four against two, but you would've never known by the way they were rumbling. That is until one of the dudes snuck up and hit Black over the head with a bottle. Sandino turned around and tossed the dude on the floor. Before he could finish handling his business, surprisingly he looked up and saw Cruze run over and instantly start stomping the dude several times. Dazed but still standing, Black watched as Sandino and Cruze took each of the dudes down.

A few minutes later, security came over and broke the fight up. Normally when club goers started commotions, everyone got put out, but in this case only the rowdy group was escorted to the door. Because Sandino and his boys always spent tons of money they were allowed to stay. Money always talked in Miami.

Once things calmed down, Sandino looked over at Cruze. "Damn, look what the muthafuckin' cat drug in," he joked.

"What up nigga?" Cruze said, hitting Sandino on the shoulder.

Black stood back and watched. He was jealous of how Sandino seemed to treat Cruze better than him. He wondered if Sandino had any plans to let Cruze back in the click that easy after the way he'd been missing over the past few months. He was the one who'd stayed around and had his back.

Black walked over to hear what they were talking about.

"What up, Black?" Cruze greeted.

"You tell me, where the fuck you been?" Black asked.

"I been chilling, sound like y'all nigga's missed me or something," Cruze replied.

"Yeah right, nigga. Let me holla at you for a minute," Sandino chimed in.

The two walked away from the crowded VIP area.

"Man, I never got a chance to apologize to you for how shit went down at that diner. You know these pills have me buggin' out sometimes. You been my man since forever and I should've never disrespected you like that. That nigga Black don't hold me down like you do, and I recognize that now," Sandino admitted.

Cruze wanted to say that it was cool, but it wasn't.

"Hopefully we can move past this. Why don't you come back and work for me," Sandino added.

"Unlike some people in your crew, I'm not interested in just working for you. I'm your friend, nigga. I was there for you way before you became a fucking football player."

"I know man, and that's why I'm apologizin' once again. I fucked up."

Cruze looked at Sandino. He'd lost so much weight since the last time they saw each other. He also wondered if Sandino was getting soft because he'd never heard his long-time friend apologize to anyone. Not even Skye. It was just something he didn't do. He felt sorry for Sandino even though the shit he did was still foul.

"Apology accepted my nigga. I knew you couldn't live without me," Cruze joked.

The two stood and talked for awhile until Reka, a chic Cruze was at the club with, walked up.

"Damn Cruze, I been walking around looking for your ass. Where you been?" she asked with an attitude.

"I'm sorry baby, go back and have a seat at the bar. I'll be right over," Cruze instructed. With all the commotion, he'd totally forgotten about Reka's fine ass.

When she walked away, Cruze and Sandino both watched her huge ass shaking in her short, BCBG freakum dress.

"Damn, who is that?" Sandino asked, drooling from the mouth.

"Somebody off limits to you playa," Cruze said laughing and walking away.

"Well, I suggest you get her outta here, cause Sandino Washington will get them drawers," he responded with a loud laugh.

When Cruze walked away, Sandino headed back over to VIP.

About an hour later, Cruze and Reka were drunk and having sex in one of the men's bathroom stalls. Reka was on her knees sucking Cruze's dick when Sandino and Black walked inside.

"I'm glad you finally snapped out of it and decided to leave the fucking house," Black said.

"Yeah, I'm startin' to lose it. Skye needs to bring her fuckin' ass home so I can see my kids."

"Well, at least we know it'll only be a matter of time before Dre finds out their whereabouts in Atlanta," Black reassured.

"He better," Sandino said, walking over to one of the urinals. "Man, why every time we come to the fuckin' club, nigga's have to test us?"

"Yeah, you right, but we went toe to toe with them young heads. I thought Cruze was a punk, but he came though for our ass tonight!" Black replied. "I gotta give his ass props."

"Fuck that nigga Cruze, especially since he wanted to go missin' in action and didn't even bother to come see me while I was locked up. That's why his dumb-ass fell for that apology. I'm gonna use his ass until I know for sure that nigga is loyal again. As a matter of fact, if Dre doesn't do a good job, I might send his ass to Atlanta, too."

"Yeah, that was foul how he just up and disappeared on you like that that. He knew you were going through some shit," Black co-signed as usual.

Cruze stood in the stall listening to Sandino shit on him once again. He waited for them to exit the bathroom then pushed Reka off him and zipped up his pants.

I'm going to show Sandino's ass what loyalty is really about, Cruze thought.

🏈🏈🏈🏈🏈🏈🏈🏈

Wearing a t-shirt and a pair of cut off shorts, Mercedes went into the refrigerator and grabbed her bottle of Kendall Jackson Chardonnay instead of the orange juice. It was nine o'clock in the morning and after pouring her a nice, tall glass, she sat back down at her computer, lit another cigarette and sipped. Seemed like all she did was drink lately. The situation with Justice had completely stressed her out, not to mention the shit going on with her sons. Surfing the web, she looked for a new job since her February rent was due in two weeks. With only three hundred dollars to her name, Mercedes wasn't much of a saver, never had been…especially since she'd hoped that Justice would've asked her and the kids to move in with him by now.

Mercedes glanced at the caller ID on her house phone when it rang. Seeing the words, *Marietta Detention Ctr*, pop up on the screen, she didn't bother to answer it. She couldn't bear to hear either of her sons complaining to her about getting out. Until she found a job, Mercedes had to figure out how to keep a roof over her head and food on the table. Unfortunately, bail money just wasn't a priority at the moment. For now, the boys had made their bed so they were going to have to lay in it.

"Shit, where's the damn money at anyway if they were selling fucking drugs," she said, blowing out some smoke.

She picked up her T-Mobile, myTouch phone and dialed Justice's cell number. She knew he wasn't going to answer, which was perfectly fine since that wasn't the purpose of her call. As soon as his voicemail came on, she quickly hit the star button to activate his voicemail. After she figured out that the passcode was his birth date, Mercedes checked his voice mail at least three times a day. It was like an obsession, she had to see who'd been calling her man.

When Mercedes realized he had a new message, she turned down the TV with her remote. A frown appeared on her face within seconds as soon as she heard Skye's voice. She listened as Skye told Justice how much she enjoyed the night they'd spent together. Skye then went on to say, she couldn't wait until their date that night. Furious, Mercedes immediately deleted the message and threw her phone across the room.

"I see right now I'm gonna have to fuck her ass up. Things were headed in the right direction with Justice and I until this bitch came along!" she yelled. "Why is she trying to come between me and my man?"

She smashed the cigarette into her cheesy, New York City tourist ashtray.

Mercedes desperately needed to see if she could find out anything about who Skye was…who she was hiding from. *Maybe if I find out who was beating her ass, maybe I can get her away from Justice before I lose him forever*.

Protecting Skye's identity was out the door at this point. While working for Justice, Mercedes learned how to search the entire country's battered shelters database, so she quickly put her snooping skills to work. Pulling up another internet browser, she typed in the domain name to the website then typed in Justice's username and password. Once she was directed to the proper page, Mercedes typed in the name Janelle Coleman, but nothing came up. Frustrated, she started tapping her long fingernails against the desk.

That bitch appeared out of no where. Where is she from, Mercedes thought. She remembered trying to pick Kareem and Jordan for some information one day as well, but never got far. *She got them bastards trained.*

As time passed, Mercedes racked her brain trying to

think of what she could do to get that bitch back for stealing her man. Then it hit her…Craigslist! She remembered one of the women who previously stayed at the shelter telling her she'd met and married the man who abused her on the popular community website.

After logging on, Mercedes looked at all the advertisements and services they had. Even though there was no longer an adult services tab, that didn't stop people from finding ways to market their services. They just did it in a disguised, clever way, which was exactly what she was about to do.

Mercedes started to laugh. "I know what I can do. Janelle is gonna regret the day she decided to take something that didn't belong to her."

Excited about the plan that was about to unfold, Mercedes went to Yahoo and created a fake email account. She then went to a porn website, stole a picture of a pretty naked black girl to help with her plan.

She went back on Craigslist, typed in Atlanta for the city, then clicked on the Personals tab titled, 'women seeking men'. After hitting the, 'sex with no strings attached' link and answering a few more general questions, she finally began typing.

SOME GIRLS LIKE IT ROUGH AND RAW…

Hi, I'm Janelle and I need a man to fulfill my fantasy. If you're into role playing, so am I. Come to my house, tie me up and fuck me hard! I'm looking for someone to punish me because I'm a naughty filthy freak. Email me if you're interested. Don't be shy…I'll be waiting.

ONLY SERIOUS INQUIRES NEED TO APPLY!

Mercedes displayed an evil and wicked grin as she hit the post button. Within minutes the fake ad had over ten responses. She couldn't believe how many horny, freaky-ass men there were in the world. She was even more surprised that Craigslist allowed people to post and respond to ads like that.

She talked to one man via email about her fantasies and

painted a mental picture of what she wanted him to do to her. The man responded with his own freaky requests, which had Mercedes shaking her head. She could tell he was one sick pervert and that's exactly what she was looking for.

After giving the man Skye's address, Mercedes smiled again.

"That bitch will never make that date. I can't wait for her to finally get what she deserves!"

Chapter Twenty~Two

Skye carefully got up from the table at the nail salon grabbing her purse and keys. She refused to mess up her freshly done French manicure. Everything was almost complete for her special date with Justice later on that night. She even managed to find a cute, cheap black dress from Rainbow, a store she would've never been caught dead in when she was living off of Sandino's money.

Heading to the car, Skye stopped and turned around when she heard someone yelling at her.

"Janelle, Janelle!"

Skye wondered who the big woman was as she walked toward her.

"Janelle, hold up for a minute!" When the woman finally approached her, she seemed out of breath. "Girl…I need to lose some damn weight."

Skye chuckled, but didn't respond.

"Don't you remember me? We were at the shelter together. My name is Toya," the woman said when Skye seemed concerned.

Skye nodded her head. "Oh…yeah that's right. I'm sorry, I guess I didn't recognize you at first."

Skye questioned what Toya could've possibly wanted.

"How you been?" Toya asked. "You look good."

"Thanks, I've been well," Skye responded.

"Well, I went by the shelter about a week ago to talk to Justice about something and he wasn't there. I asked Mercedes if she knew where he was and she said, with a crazy look in her eyes, probably with that bitch, Janelle."

"Oh really. That's not surprising. You know she didn't care for me very much."

"I know so that's why I just wanted to tell you once again to watch Mercedes. Before I moved out of the shelter I used to watch how jealous she got whenever she saw you and Justice together. It was obvious that Justice liked you…everybody knew it. After you got there, he started walking around smiling like he'd won the damn lottery."

Skye smiled.

"Let me tell you this one last thing and I'm not gonna hold you any longer. It was a girl who came to the shelter about a month before you got there. She was cute, but still wasn't any comparison to you. Anyway…Mercedes thought the girl liked Justice, and do you know what she did?"

"What?" Skye questioned with concern.

"Mercedes put something in that girl's food. One night after we ate, that girl woke up with shortness of breath, she was throwing up like crazy and even her nose started bleeding. Nobody suspected Mercedes, but I know that bitch did something. Hell, she was the one who went out and got us food from Olive Garden that night."

Skye was shocked but not surprised. She knew Mercedes wasn't playing with a full deck.

"Damn, that's crazy."

"Somebody need to check that bitch," Toya replied.

"Well, thanks again for the warning," Skye said opening the car door. "I really appreciate it."

"You welcome, but watch your back, because that chick got it bad for Justice."

"Okay, I certainly will," Skye replied getting into the car.

She didn't know or trust Toya well enough to discuss Mercedes any further.

While driving home she could hardly wait to see what Justice had planned for them. He'd decided to take Skye out and cheer her up after learning that she'd been fired from her job for abruptly leaving that day. He also offered to pay Lydia an extra fee to keep Payton over night while they went out.

She'd lost all confidence in herself. The fear of not having a job and needing to provide for her children along with starting a new life was intense. That's the reason Skye stayed with Sandino as long as she did. Staying in an abusive relationship with him seemed more comfortable than leaving and not knowing where she would go or how she would make ends meet. She'd been abused to the point where Skye was convinced that she was unworthy and unlovable. That's until she met Justice.

After pulling up at her apartment, Skye jumped out of the car with a giddy smile. It felt like she was going to the prom as opposed to a simple date. Even though she and Justice spent time together, most of the time it was in the house so it had been a while since she'd really gone out and enjoyed herself. Instead of picking her up from home, Skye planned to meet Justice back at the shelter since he had a lot of paper work to catch up on. She was glad he'd finally fired Mercedes ass. The thought of having to deal with that bitch on a daily basis made her skin crawl especially after talking to Toya.

Walking in the house, Skye kicked off her shoes and walked into the kitchen. She then looked at the clock on the stove. It was 1:45 p.m. and Kareem was due home from school within the next two hours. Jordan normally stayed after for basketball practice. Skye was grateful that Justice had gotten the lawyer he'd dealt with in past to somehow perform a miracle and get Kareem's house arrest conditions changed, which seemed to make her son a little less depressed. Even though he had to come straight home, at least now Kareem was able to get out of the house. She only hoped that the same lawyer could help in his case when he went to court in March.

Opening the refrigerator, Skye realized that she'd forgotten to pack Payton's apple juice that morning, so she grabbed the bottle knowing Lydia might need it. After slipping on a pair of flip flops, Skye quickly opened the door.

The excitement that she had earlier quickly turned into panic when she found a stranger standing there. The tall, olive toned man wore a baseball hat pulled down almost covering his eyes. He also had a creepy smile on his face as he stood silent in front of her.

"Can I help you?" Skye asked nervously.

She knew most of her neighbors, so the Italian looking guy didn't seem familiar.

"Of course you can Janelle. You sent me a message saying you wanted to be tied up, spanked and raped. So here I am," he said, with a little snicker.

Skye's eyes widened. *How the fuck does he know that name*, she thought.

Realizing something wasn't right, she quickly tried to close the door. Thinking it was all part of an act, the man took his right shoulder and pushed the door open before coming inside.

"Oh, I like playing games like this. Come here, baby. Come to big daddy," he said, holding his hands out and walking toward her.

His huge two hundred and forty pound hairy body made him look more like a gorilla than a human and he had the kind of face that would make milk turn sour.

"Get away from me!" Skye yelled, as she grabbed a lamp off the table by the door and threw it at him. But as luck would have it, his fat-ass managed to dodge the flying piece of furniture. "Get the hell out of my house!" She screamed to the top of her lungs hoping someone would hear her.

Skye took off running, trying to get to her bedroom

closet. She'd purchased a gun without anyone knowing two days after thinking she saw Cruze. Not even Justice knew the small .25 caliber handgun was in one of her shoe boxes. Even though it wasn't registered, it was still protection.

Allowing her to only get a few feet away, the intruder ran behind Skye grabbing a hold of her hair and pushing her to the floor. Skye fought him hard, throwing several blows to his face knocking the baseball hat off. His hair was greasy, like he'd put a ton of gel in it.

"Yeah…that's what I'm talking bout. Fighting back makes my dick harder."

"Stop it!" Skye yelled.

She struggled to break away, but to no avail as he positioned himself on top of her confining her body to the floor.

"Please…please…don't rape me," she begged.

"Shut up!" he roared.

When Skye realized she wouldn't be able to get him off of her, she took her fingernails and dug them deep into his skin scratching his arms and left cheek. Yelling from the pain, he took his fist and punched her in the face twice. It was like being with Sandino all over again.

"Get off of me!"

When she screamed, the intruder placed his hands over her mouth then grabbed a sock and roll of duck tape out of his jacket pocket. He seemed well prepared. After stuffing the sock in her mouth, he then placed two pieces of tape over her lips. It was just like a scene out of a movie.

He pulled out a knife and stuck it to her face. "If you move, I'll kill you," the intruder said, tying up her hands. As he wrapped his huge hands around her entire neck, he looked down at her with crazed eyes. "Why are you looking at me like that? You wanted this, so I came, bitch."

Placing the knife on the floor, he stuck his tongue out and started licking her face with his nasty smelling breath. Skye felt like she was about to throw up. Her muffled screams and struggling, of course, excited him even more.

"No one will hear you. There will be no interruptions or salvation for you cunt. This is mine to do with as I please," the intruder bragged.

Standing over her body, he grabbed the top of her sweatpants then pulled them off. With her multi print bikini panties exposed, he smiled.

"Nice thighs," he said, rubbing his rough hands down her legs.

His blood pumped harder causing his dick to swell. He almost went insane from the excitement of seeing this helpless woman squirm and beg for help, but her writhes and squirms in a vain attempt to break free were useless.

"That's right bitch…put up a fight," he said.

After ripping off her panties, he took off his tan, uniform looking Dockers pants along with his boxers then spread her legs apart. When Skye started kicking her legs, he punched her in the face again. This time it was a forceful kind of blow that left her in a daze. She could taste the blood in her mouth. Within seconds, he'd lunged his dick inside her dry pussy. Skye moaned in horrific pain when she felt his huge tool moving in and out non-stop. It felt like her coochie was on fire.

Skye laid in a daze as he pounded away and licked her face. Tears welled up in her eyes at the thought of a strange man inside her body and when he whispered in her ear over and over, "You wanted this so I came."

He looked into her eyes as his thickening raping tool continued it's vigorous plunges. Over and over he would repeatedly thrust in and out of her pussy. He reveled at the fact that she was not only in extreme pain, but was also in absolute despair. Skye felt completely violated.

When she heard him moan and start to pumping even harder, Skye thought he was about to have an orgasm and it would all be over. But she was wrong, he was just getting started.

"I guess you want it in the ass now…huh?"

Hearing him say that really made Skye struggle to break free. Laughing, he rolled Skye over on her stomach and then pulled her thighs apart taking aim at her rectum. Once again he hurled his solid dick deep where it didn't belong. Her muted screams rang out throughout the room as he unmercifully pumped in and out of her struggling body, while grabbing and squeezing her ass cheeks. Her body felt numb. Grunting with the effort of every thrust, he raped her harder…faster…over and over … until he exploded.

But he wasn't done yet. He pulled his still hard dick out, pent her legs back and entered her again. He continued to rape her for another thirty minutes until she felt his body shiver and he released all over her stomach.

He didn't even wear a condom, was all she kept thinking.

Skye prayed he didn't have AIDS or any other STD as he removed himself from in between her legs and smiled.

"Damn, that pussy was better than I thought it would be. Let me know when you want another fantasy fulfilled and I'll gladly come back," he said, pulling up his pants and walking out the door.

Skye laid naked, on the floor thinking, *I just wanna die.*

Jackie D.

Chapter Twenty~Three 🏈

Dre spent half the day driving around Atlanta asking questions about Skye, but nobody seemed to know who she was. He couldn't believe how things had changed since he was locked up. He rode through The Bowen Homes Housing projects where he used to sell drugs and was totally taken aback when he realized it had been demolished. When he ran into some of his old homeboys they filled him in on how the destruction of the projects was part of the city's plan to get rid of what officials say had become one of the worst crime-infested public housing developments.

"Where the fuck is Deuce at? That nigga ain't been around here gamblin' in months," a guy named Slick stated.

"He doin' other shit now," Dre responded.

"I miss winnin' all that niggas dough," Slick added.

Dre continued standing on the corner reminiscing and listening to them talk about a group of new drug dealers that called themselves, Black Mafia Family or BMF for short. Apparently they were making loads of money and were known to flash around town in tricked-out motorcycles, Bentley Coupes and iced out jewelry.

"And the bitches in the strip club love them niggas. When they come up in the spot, you can forget about getting a damn lap dance," Slick carried on.

After getting tired of hearing about how much money

those niggas were getting, Dre cut the visit short. He didn't want to be tempted to re-live his days of hustling. He said his goodbyes and jumped into his car and headed downtown on Peachtree Street. After riding for a few minutes, he stopped at a light and looked up at the Ritz Carlton.

Sandino got me looking on the street, and she's probably laid up in a nice-ass hotel suite compliments of his ass, Dre thought.

Suddenly, Dre's phone rang, starling him. When he looked at the screen and saw Sandino's name he became agitated. Sandino had just called not to long ago and it was pissing Dre off. He hesitated before answering. Dre knew Sandino would be mad that he didn't have any leads yet. On the other hand, if he didn't answer it Sandino would think he'd played him so he decided to answer it. Dre took a deep breath.

"Hello."

"Have you found out anything yet?" Sandino asked.

"Not yet. I'm out in the streets lookin' and askin', but nobody has seen her. I hit a few flea bag motels, and even went to all the homeless shelters in town. Nobody has seen a woman named Skye wit' three kids. I guess it's gonna take a lil' longer."

Sandino was high as hell and started going off and yelling in the phone instantly. "What the fuck you mean not yet? I thought you said you were from Atlanta and once you hit the street you would know something on her whereabouts?"

"I'm on it, but 'dis shit ain't easy. I don't even have a picture."

"It shouldn't be that hard. That bitch don't have no money or family there, so it can't be that difficult. I paid you to find her ass. I need this shit done now or else I'm gonna send Black down there to get my fuckin' money back. I'll get somebody else to do the job if you can't handle it. Or if need be, I'll come down there and find the bitch myself!" Sandino belted. "Have you tried the schools? Both of my boys are in high school. I'm pretty sure she's registered them by now."

"Are you jokin'? Do you know how many high schools are in Atlanta?"

"Well at least I'm tryin' to come up wit' different options. It doesn't look like you're doin' shit," Sandino criticized.

"Look Sandino, I just got here two days ago and I told you I'm on it. Don't call me wit' no fuckin' threats, I'm not one of your lil' flunkies. I'll have somethin' for you in a few days!" Dre said, then hung up the phone. "I don't know who the fuck 'dat nigga think he talkin' to," Dre mumbled to himself.

Dre was so pissed at the way Sandino tried to handle him on the phone. For a second he contemplated calling the whole thing off, and keeping the money he already had, but thought about the rest of the money and what he could do with it to get back on his feet.

After riding around and coming up empty, he checked into the Marriott Marquis on Peachtree Center Avenue. After staying at and being dissatisfied at a Hilton Garden Inn the night before, he hoped this hotel was better. Dre wished he could've stayed with his brother, but didn't feel like having Justice continuously judge him.

Once Dre grabbed his bag from the car he went inside the hotel and checked in.

"Sir, I need to see a valid ID," the front desk agent said.

Dre was staring at her double D breasts and plump lips so hard he didn't hear a word she said.

"Sir, are you okay?" the woman asked loudly.

She was a cutie, but Dre could tell she was ghetto as hell by the bright blonde weave she wore.

"Oh yeah, sorry," he said, shaking his head.

"Your ID and a credit card please."

"Oh…okay," he said, reaching into his back pocket. He pulled out his driver's license and handed it to her. "I don't have a credit card though."

"I'll need one for incidentals sir," the agent replied.

Dre reached into his pocket and pulled out a hundred dollar bill. He had to do the same thing at the last hotel. "You think we could forget about the credit card. I promise I won't be rentin' any dirty movies or orderin' room service," he said, sliding the bill.

The agent turned her head both ways before slipping the money in her pocket. "No problem."

While waiting for her to check him in, Dre looked over at the revolving door when he heard the sound of kids running in the hotel. He saw a woman with two kids along with a baby in a stroller walk into the lobby. He wondered if that could possibly be Skye. She was fine and fit the description that Sandino had given him. He continued watching as she made her way over to the front desk. They made eye contact before she started talking to the young woman at the desk.

"Hello Mrs. Raines, are you enjoying your time in town?" the front desk agent asked.

"Yes, I like it here. In fact if my husband closes this deal today, we'll be packing up our home in New York and moving all our lil' crumb snatchers here. We never wanted to raise our kids in New York anyway," she replied.

The desk agent smiled. "Well, welcome to Atlanta in advance."

A few minutes later a man walked in with two more kids.

"Thanks, keep your fingers crossed that we close on that deal," Mrs. Raines replied as the couple and their Brady Bunch headed to the hotel's restaurant.

I guess 'dat wasn't Skye, he thought.

Once the woman checked him in, she handed him his key. Dre smiled at her as he walked away from the counter and headed to the elevator.

When Dre got to room 304, he stuck the key in the door and opened it. He then sat his bag in a corner then plopped down on the bed. With the remote in hand he flipped through the channels.

"Damn, ain't shit interestin' on," he said, landing on The Dr. Oz Show.

Since Dre couldn't find anything to watch, he decided to catch up on some sleep. He scooped up one of the pillows and stuck it behind his head. After staring at the ceiling trying to figure out how he was going to find Skye for about ten minutes, it suddenly hit him.

Sitting back up, Dre grabbed his cell phone off the night stand. He decided to call Mercedes for help even though he was hesitant after the conversation with Justice. It was obvious that she was two short of a six pack now, but at this point, he didn't have anything to lose.

He dialed her number not knowing what mood she was going to be in.

"What the fuck do you want now, Dre?" Mercedes asked as soon as she answered.

"Hey Mercedes, I was just callin' to check on you."

"Well, I should be so lucky. I'm just sitting trying to decide who to invite to the wedding. I'm pissed that your brother is acting a little stupid right now, but I know he'll come around, so I'm moving forward with the plans."

Dre laughed to himself. He started to ask who the hell was going to be her maid of honor since he now knew the real story, but he needed her help, so he played it cool and went along with the story.

"So, what's up?" she asked.

"I need your help wit' findin' somebody."

"What makes you think I can help you do something like that?"

"Because I thought since you worked at the shelter you might have information about the people who've stayed there. Plus I know about 'dat database for all the shelters 'dat Justice has access to, and wondered if you did, too."

"So, since your ass just said, *worked*, you must know that he fired me."

"Yeah, I do."

"What did that bastard say?"

"Look, I don't wanna get into 'dat right now. He didn't say anything bad," Dre lied. "So, can you help."

"Maybe…maybe not. What's in it for me?" she asked.

Dre shook his head, *some things never change,* he thought. "I'll slide you some change if you can help."

"I saw the wad of money you had in your pocket Dre. I need at least four hundred dollars."

"Aight."

"What do you need help with?"

"Have you heard anything about Sandino Washington's wife bein' in town?"

"Who the fuck is Sandino Washington?"

Dre laughed. He suddenly remembered that Mercedes didn't know anything about sports.

"He's an ex NFL player who played for the Miami Dolphins."

"Oh, no, but why are you interested in Sandino Washington's wife? Are you fucking her or something?"

"No, but she took his kids and he wants them back. He payin' top dollar to find her."

"Really. Well, I can call my girl Nessa. All the celebrities who come to town go to her salon. If she's here, Nessa will know about it."

"Ummm. I don't think his wife would really wanna be out there getting' her hair done. If anything she would be hidin' out. That's why I was wonderin' if you could look in 'dat database. Maybe she's stayin' at a shelter," Dre informed.

Mercedes walked over to her computer that was already on and sat down. She had plans on logging into the shelter's database, but decided to do something else first. "Let's see what she looks like," Mercedes said.

She wanted the get her hands on some of that money too. After going to Goggle, she typed in, *Sandino Washington NFL player*, then waited for the results. After clicking on images, a few seconds later, a picture of him, Skye and the kids popped on her screen.

Mercedes gasped. "Oh my God!"

"What's wrong?" Dre asked.

"Ummm, nothing," Mercedes said.

She didn't want Dre to contact Sandino. In her mind, she wanted to contact him herself.

"I gotta go!"

CLICK!

🏈🏈🏈🏈🏈🏈🏈

Skye sat on the side of a hospital bed in the emergency room with Justice holding her hand and apologizing for not being there to protect her. Her body ached, her face was badly bruised, and she had a huge knot on her forehead. But nothing compared to her nervousness. Skye hadn't stopped shaking since she arrived and jumped every time the nurse entered the room. She wondered why a dark cloud always seemed to follow her.

Along with being upset about her horrific experience, Skye was also saddened about Kareem coming home from school and finding her naked and tied up on the floor. After covering her up, he called 911 and stayed by her side until the paramedics arrived. Skye hadn't seen Kareem cry in months, but once he found out what happened, he couldn't help but shed a few tears as his mother sobbed uncontrollably. With him being on restricted house arrest, Kareem was disappointed after realizing he couldn't escort her to the hospital, but Skye assured him she would be okay. She needed him to step up and be the man of the house for Jordan and Payton.

Skye looked up and wiped her eyes when a female doctor walked in.

"Mrs. Coleman, I'm Dr. Devoe, How are you feeling?"

"Numb," was all Skye could say in regards to how she felt.

"I know you've been through a traumatic experience and I want to make this examination as quick as possible," Dr. Devoe explained. She looked at Justice. "I'm gonna have to ask you to leave the room if you don't mind."

He kissed Skye on the head. "I'll be right outside if you need me baby," he said walking out the room.

Moments later, a nurse appeared and helped the doctor as she prepared to do the rape kit on Skye. The nurse helped Skye to her feet and onto a large piece of paper draped on the floor right beside the bed.

"I need you to undress right here and lay back down on top of the bed," the doctor ordered.

The nurse then covered the hospital bed with the same type of paper. She later explained that the paper was used to catch any fibers or hairs that would be collected during the exam so they could be placed into the rape kit.

"I need you to open your legs and place them in the stir-ups please. This will be quick," Dr. Devoe reassured her again in a gentle tone.

Skye opened her legs and did as she was told, but closed her eyes when she had a vision of the man raping her. When she began to shake non-stop, the nurse walked over and rubbed her arm.

"I know this is hard for you, but we have to do this so we can hopefully catch this animal and put him away."

"Okay," Skye managed to say.

A few seconds later, the doctor grabbed a small kit and started combing Skye's pubic area for possible hair samples. After that was done, she scraped underneath her nails to collect tissue samples. She would stop every few minutes and drop the samples into a container and label it with Skye's name. She then took an ultraviolet light and scanned her entire body trying to locate semen or saliva. After the vaginal exam was over, she pulled out a camera and took pictures of all the bruises.

"Okay, all done. We just need a blood and urine sample and I'll give you some medication to treat any potential STD's since you're concerned that the rapist didn't use a condom. We'll contact you once we get your results back from the lab," the doctor stated.

"Thanks," Skye responded.

Once the doctor left the room, the nurse checked Skye's IV and changed the bandage on her head.

"Are you okay, Mrs. Colman? Is there anything else I can get you before I leave?" the nurse asked.

"I'll be okay."

"Well, buzz me if you change your mind. Also, just so you know, the hospital will provide you with information to a rape crisis center for counseling if you need it," she said, leaving the room.

A few seconds later Justice peeked his head in the door. "Baby, there're some officers out here in the hall who need to ask you a few questions."

"Can you tell them to come back later? I don't feel like talking right now."

"Baby, I know you're still upset, but you might as well get it over with."

After giving it some thought, she knew Justice was right. "Alright. Tell them to come in."

Skye fixed her hair and tried to get herself together before the officers entered the room, one of which was a female.

"Hello, I'm Officer Smythe and this is Officer Jenkins," he said pointing to the female.

"For the record, can you state your name?" the officer asked with a pad in his hand.

Skye broke down and immediately started crying. She wanted so badly to give them her real name, but gave them the fake name instead.

"Janelle Coleman."

"We just need to ask you a few questions about what happened to you. We were able to get a sample of the semen for the DNA testing. Did you by any chance know the man that raped you?"

"No, I didn't know him. I'm new to the area and don't know many people here."

The officers both looked at Justice like they were wondering what his relationship to Skye was, but didn't bother asking. After several other questions, they finished up.

"Mrs. Coleman, once you're released we'll come to your house and dust for finger prints."

"Okay," Skye replied. For some reason she started to breakdown.

When they left, Skye continued to cry. Justice walked up and consoled her.

"Janelle I want you and the boys to move in with me so I can protect you."

She lowered her head before speaking. "Justice, I have to decline because if I agree to move in with you, Kareem will probably have an issue with that. I just can't risk it. I'm already having problems with him."

"Well, if you can't move in with me, then what about me moving in with you?"

After thinking about it, surprisingly, Skye agreed. She looked over at his handsome face and decided it was time to tell him who she really was.

"Justice, I have something to tell you. She broke down again. "I'm so tired of running, lying and being scared. My name isn't Janelle Coleman, it's Skye Washington. My husband's name is Sandino Washington who used to play for the Miami Dolphins. I can't keep living my life like this," she dropped her head and wailed.

Her name sounded so familiar. *Skye Washington...Skye Washington. Oh, wait that's the name Dre asked me about the other day. I wonder what's the connection,* Justice wondered. *But he mentioned something about green eyes.*

He stared at Skye. "So, is that your real eye color?"

Skye shook her head. "No, I've been getting these fake contacts from a beauty supply this whole time. My eyes are really green. It was all a cover-up, but I'm tired of that, too."

"It's okay baby, I love you regardless of who you are. I'm just glad you finally told me the truth." Justice lifted her head. "I like the name Skye better anyway. Do you think we can get a hook up on some tickets to a Dolphins game," he joked.

Since she'd finally decided to come clean, Justice desperately wanted to tell her about the night with Mercedes and even his wife, but still didn't think it was the appropriate time.

Ain't no sense in making her even more upset, he thought. In *the meantime, I've gotta find out what Dre wanted with her.*

Chapter Twenty~Four 🏈

Kareem stood in the small, cramped, smoke-filled kitchen trying to prepare a meal for the family. On the menu were peas, boxed macaroni and cheese along with some spaghetti noodles with tomato sauce. He'd watched Ms. Petra prepare their meals for years and it looked easy, so he decided to take a chance.

Kareem stirred the noodles trying to keep them from sticking to the bottom of the pot, but wasn't having much luck. The kitchen was a complete mess and it smelled like burnt food, but he was determined to have a nice, hot meal when his mother returned home from the hospital. He was in a good mood, and had already cleaned up the apartment so Skye didn't have anything to do once she arrived. He just wanted her to relax.

The vision of him walking in the house and finding his mother laying on the floor naked, badly beaten and tied up was still etched in his mind. After calling 911, he constantly asked Skye who'd done that to her, but her response was the same each time, "I don't know." He wanted to kill whoever had the audacity to touch his mother.

When the paramedics arrived, Skye made Kareem promise that he would take care of Jordan and Payton while she was gone. She also asked him not to tell Jordan what happened. Skye definitely didn't want him to know anything about the incident. She wanted to tell him on her own time, if she said anything at all.

Kareem remembered snapping out of his frantic state of mind once the ambulance pulled off and realized he needed to step up and be the man like he promised he would be when they first left Miami. The one thing he admired about his mother was how she was always able to remain strong and keep moving forward, no matter what she went through. Now, it was finally time to make her proud.

When Kareem heard his favorite song, *6', 7'* by Little Wayne, he threw down the fork he was using and turned up the small portable radio. He began rapping along with the lyrics and even displayed a few hand gestures, imitating the New Orleans native MC.

At that moment, Jordan walked into the kitchen holding Payton. He looked at the food frowning up his face then started waving his hand back and forth from all the smoke. He walked over and cut on the fan over top of the stove.

"Damn, I was wondering where that shit was," Kareem joked.

"Why are you in here trying to cook? You've never cooked a day in your life. This don't even go together, where's Ma?" Jordan inquired.

"Stop asking so many questions, she'll be home shortly. She asked me to look out for you and Payton, so I'm cooking some food, it's almost ready."

Jordan frowned again. "I'm not gonna eat that food. You haven't even been around, now all of a sudden you wanna play big brother and cook? Ma doesn't fix no nasty food like this."

Kareem got mad and started throwing the plates down on the counter. He knew Jordan was right, but refused to admit it in front of his little brother.

"Jordan shut up before I choke your ungrateful-ass out!" Kareem yelled.

"I'm not eating that food. I'm ordering a pizza with the emergency money Ma keeps in her shoebox. I know it's in her closet."

"Yes, you are going to eat this food. Ma told me to make sure y'all eat and that's what I'm doing! She left me in charge!" Kareem began to shout.

"No, I'm not. You don't scare me Kareem. I can smack you right now and run down the street and you can't even chase me with that house arrest thing on your ankle." Jordan pointed toward Kareem's leg. "You need to get your mind right. All you do is think about yourself. Ma doesn't deserve a son like you especially after dealing with Daddy all those years," Jordan said walking out the kitchen.

Kareem started piling the nasty looking macaroni and cheese onto the plates. Hearing Jordan's words cut him deep because again it was the truth.

"Little asshole," Kareem mumbled to himself before sitting the pot back down. "Let me go hide that box before he really tries to order a pizza."

Walking down the hall, Kareem noticed Jordan rocking Payton to sleep when he passed their room. When he entered his mother's closet, he looked up on the top shelf forgetting which of the three shoe boxes the money was in. After grabbing the first box and only seeing Skye's sneakers, he proceeded to the next one. What Kareem saw inside the second box, instantly made his eyes enlarge.

"Oh my God," Kareem said, picking up the pistol. He'd seen Sandino flash his gun on several occasions, but had yet to actually hold a firearm. "I can't believe she has this and didn't say anything about this."

As Kareem examined the weapon, he suddenly heard his mother coming through the door.

"Oh shit," he said putting the gun back in the box.

He quickly made his way back into the living room just as Skye took off her coat. She smiled, noticing that the apartment was extra clean, but wondered what the horrible smell was when both of the boys walked over and embraced her.

"Where's Payton?" Skye inquired.

"She just went to sleep. She's laying on my bed. Ma, what happened? Did Dad do this to you?" Jordan asked as soon as he noticed her face. He got really upset.

As Jordan observed Skye, Kareem eye-balled Justice. He hated that Justice was around so much.

Skye really didn't want to explain what happened to her fourteen year old son, but thought he had a right to know. "Sit down Jordan and let me explain."

The two sat down as Skye tried to get herself together.

"This afternoon, I was on my way over to Lydia's when a man approached me. He looked at me real strange and when I turned to run back into the apartment, he chased me and forced his way inside."

"So, what happened?" Jordan asked with a curious expression.

Skye tried to swallow the lump in her throat. "Well, me and the man…we fought a little, but he was too strong and he ended up raping me."

Jordan frowned. "Raped you? What does that mean?"

"I know your Dad talked to you a little bit about sex, so rape means when one person forces the other person to have sex with them. In this case, the man forced me," Skye struggled to say.

"Are you okay, Ma? Did they catch him? Do you think Daddy sent the man?" Jordan hysterically asked.

"I'm okay baby. I don't know if your Dad had anything to do with this, but it's not his style," Skye replied. *The last thing he would want to do is share me with another man*, she thought.

Justice interrupted. "Your mother is a brave woman. She was able to get some of the intruder's skin under her nails. Once they run his DNA in the system they might be able to catch him."

Kareem reached over and hugged Skye. "I'm so sorry this happened to you. I should've never gone to school. I should've stayed at home so I could protect you."

"Don't blame yourself Kareem, it's not your fault. Justice is moving in with us for protection, so you don't have to worry about that anymore," Skye informed.

Kareem instantly whipped his head around like the little girl in *The Exorcist*. "Naawww, fuck that. Where was he when you got raped? He should've been here. What kind of protection is he? He can't live here!"

Skye instantly broke down and started crying uncontrollably. "Kareem please, stop it! I can't take anymore stress. Why can't you just accept that fact that I'm happy with Justice? I'm trying to move on with my life and make it better for all of us."

"Because you don't need another man to take care of you! What if he starts beating you like our father did?" Kareem shot back.

"My life is a mess. Maybe that man should've just killed me." With tears streaming down her face, Skye ran into her room and slammed the door.

"I told you Kareem. You always thinking of yourself!" Jordan yelled then walked away.

Kareem ignored his brother as he looked over at Justice with rage filled eyes. "Why don't you just leave us the hell alone? I'm the man of the house now. We don't need you or another father!"

Justice was sick of Kareem's mouth. So he finally said something slick back to him. "I'm not trying to be your crazy-ass father."

Kareem had a surprised look formed on his face.

"Yeah, your mother finally told me who you are. Kareem Washington, right? Sandino Washington is your father. Well, let's get something straight right now. I've kept my mouth closed long enough. I'm gonna be the man of the house from now on, and it ain't shit you can do about it. You got it?"

"Get the fuck outta here. I don't have to listen to you!" Kareem yelled.

"You will listen if you plan to stay in this house. We can get along or I can make your life real difficult. It's up to you. I just want to make your mother is happy and you're in the fucking way of me doing that."

Kareem looked at Justice again. The two stood, ice grilling each other before Kareem asked, "Is that a threat?"

"Take it however you want lil' nigga!" Justice replied.

🏈🏈🏈🏈🏈🏈🏈

"Shut the fuck up bitch!" he said, smacking Skye in the face.

He rolled her over on her stomach and then pulled her thighs apart before plunging his thick dick deep into her pussy. Her muffled screams rang out throughout the room as he unmercifully fucked in and out of her struggling body.

"No," Skye tried to scream. "Please stop."

"How does it feel Janelle? Does it feel good to you? You wanted this, so I came bitch!"

Just as he was about to smack Skye again, she sat straight up in the bed and screamed to the top of her lungs. Gasping for air, sweat suddenly began to race down her face as Justice jumped up and tried to calm her down. She was shaking so bad, he could barely hold onto her body.

"It's okay baby. It was probably just a bad dream," Justice said, stroking her hair.

"But he called me Janelle…he called me Janelle," she kept repeating as Justice held her.

"What are you talking about?"

"The man who raped me, he kept calling me Janelle. How did he know that name?"

Crying, Skye still couldn't believe that this had happened to her. The whole experience left her confused and emotionally drained. Like her life was spinning out of control. Violated by a man who was still out there somewhere. Every time Skye thought about it, she would get mad as hell. Justice tried to assure her that she was safe and that everything was going to be alright, but Skye wasn't so sure about that, especially since they had no idea who the man was or how he knew her name. Something just wasn't adding up.

"The only people who knew I went by Janelle are the people at the shelter." She quickly pulled from Justice. "Did you have something to do with this?"

Justice's eyes damn near popped out of his head. "I can't believe you would even ask me something like that. You really think I'm capable of doing something that horrible to you…to any woman for that matter?" he asked. "I'm not some type of animal."

Skye wiped her face and then looked into his eyes. She could tell that her question had insulted him.

"I'm sorry. I've been around you long enough to know you wouldn't do something so evil. I'm just grasping at straws."

"It's okay. I know you're under a lot of stress, but I would never do something like that."

"I just want to put this out of my mind and get on with my life, but I can't."

"Of course you can't. It just happened today. It's too soon to try and forget."

Skye sat quietly for awhile not even acknowledging what Justice was saying. *So, who was evil enough to do something so vile? Was it Sandino*, she thought. *No, he would never want another man touching me. Besides, he has no idea what name I was using.* After eliminating her soon to be ex-husband, it hit her.

"Justice, I know exactly who sent that man."

"Who?"

"That bitch Mercedes," she stated with confidence.

When Skye first said it, Justice thought she was being irrational; but after giving it some thought himself, he knew she had a point. Mercedes had been acting crazy lately and she was definitely jealous of their relationship.

"You know what, it's because of you that bitch did this shit," Skye suddenly said.

Justice's eyebrows crinkled. "What?"

"You heard me. It's because of you. Why would she do something like this if something hadn't happened between the two of you? Be honest...have you ever fucked her?"

Justice tried to dodge the question. "Skye please..."

"Answer the question. Did you fuck her?"

Justice lowered his head. "Yes, but I swear on my mother's life, it was only once."

Skye looked like she wanted to cry, but went off instead. "Get the fuck out. I don't ever wanna see your face again. This shit is all your fault!"

She jumped off the bed, grabbed his clothes and overnight bag then threw them out of her room.

"Skye, please calm down," he pleaded. "I had nothing to do with this."

By this time, Payton started crying from her crib.

"Get...out!"

Justice tried his best to talk to her, but Skye wouldn't hear of it. As far as she was concerned, he was just as guilty as Mercedes was.

"Skye, I promise you, I'll get to the bottom of this if it was her."

"For the last time, get the hell out!" Skye screamed, as she pushed him out of her room.

After she slammed the door in his face, Justice grabbed his belongings. Kareem who was awakened by his mother's screams, stood in the hallway on his way to her room when Justice came walking past slowly. All Kareem could do was smile.

"And don't bring your ass back here either," Kareem said, following him to the door.

Jackie D.

Chapter Twenty-Five

"Damn girl!" Dre moaned as Mercedes bounced up and down on his rock hard dick.

She rode him like a true stallion. Her wet, shaved pussy grinded him hard and deep, showing off her professional pornographic skills. With his hands around her small waist, Dre was mesmerized at how sexy she was. Her hair was pulled up in a ponytail and the long pair of pearls she wore around her neck laid right between her large breasts.

She always did know how to ride 'dis dick, Dre thought watching Mercedes do her thing.

A few minutes later, Mercedes leaned over and started kissing him passionately.

"Ooohhh, Baby Girl you feel so damn good," Dre mumbled in between their kisses.

She continued to bounce on him making her ass jiggle out of control. Hornier than ever, Dre squeezed her ass then fucked her back with long, deep strokes. His dick throbbed as her tight pussy cried for more and her hips moved to the perfect rhythm.

"You tryna drive a nigga crazy, huh?" Dre asked as he struggled to catch his breath.

"You know once my pussy hits this good ass dick, its magic baby," Mercedes said back to him.

After several minutes of grinding, Mercedes felt herself

about to cum.

"Oh shit, I'm cummming Dre, cum with me baby," she begged.

Like a trained student, Dre started pumping faster which caused her to let out a huge scream followed by a moan.

"I'm cummmin' too!" Dre yelled, releasing along with her.

Within seconds, the two embraced tightly before collapsing on the queen-size bed panting.

Mercedes smiled to herself thinking, *part one of my plan has worked. Now I need to put part two in effect.*

She'd sweet talked Dre into coming over her house earlier that day by telling him she had some news about Skye. When he arrived, she was dressed in a sexy black negligee, sipping on a glass of wine with some slow music playing in the background. Mercedes knew Dre couldn't resist her. Despite the fact that it was only twelve o'clock in the afternoon, she still managed to get him tipsy before proceeding to seduce him. Soon, they were having some good mid-day sex. Obviously, he'd forgotten all about the news concerning Skye.

Dre's loud cell phone ringing from his pants pocket on the floor instantly caught her attention. Dre ignored it at first, but when it kept ringing his facial expression changed. He reached over and grabbed his pants. When Dre looked at the number, he hopped straight up and answered it.

"What up man?" he asked walking out the bedroom.

Mercedes admired Dre's nice body, and even more so his big, thick dick. She had to admit Dre was fine and could fuck his ass off, but nothing or nobody compared to Justice. He was gonna be her man by any means necessary.

Snapping out of her daze, Mercedes suddenly remembered her initial plan. She jumped up and stood at the door eavesdropping on Dre's call. When she heard him say, "Sandino, I think I have a lead. I'll call you back in about an hour." Mercedes knew what she had to do.

She quickly ran back in the bed and waited for Dre to get off the phone. When he came back into the bedroom, she put her acting skills to work.

"Dre baby, come here," she said in a sexy tone. When he walked over and sat next to her on the bed, she kissed his hand. "Baby, I don't want this sex marathon to end. Can you run to the store and get some candles. I want it a little more romantic around here. I got some more tricks up my sleeve for your ass!"

A huge smile formed on Dre's face. No matter how hard he tried, he couldn't resist Mercedes. He couldn't believe he'd been over her house that long and she had yet to mention Justice.

Maybe she finally got over her delusional thoughts of them getting married, he thought.

Either way as long as she was willing to give him some pussy he was going to take it.

"Yeah, I can do 'dat. Let me take a shower first though. My balls are a lil' sticky," he joked.

Dre headed to the bathroom forgetting all about his phone laying on the night stand. As soon as the coast was clear, Mercedes picked up his cell phone, looked at the number from the last call, and wrote it down.

"Let part two of the plan begin," she said to herself.

๑๑๑๑๑๑๑๑

Dripped in diamonds and dressed in a Gucci shirt and matching Gucci loafers, Sandino walked into the drug rehabilitation class dreading having to sit through his first lecture on how drugs destroy your life. Not thoroughly understanding how his addiction not only led to the demise of his career, but also the loss of his family and many of his friends, he didn't understand what the fuss was all about. So he took a few pills and snorted coke here and there, what was the harm?

He plopped down in the seat and looked around the

brightly lit room complete with coffee and donuts. The group was filled with former and present drug addicts. Most of them were prescription abusers like Sandino, but many others were heroin and crack addicts.

Moments later, the counselor, a white man in his fifties asked everyone for their attention so he could start the meeting. He soon opened up the floor to anyone who wanted to share their experience. Moving around in his seat, Sandino became agitated when a man stood up and started to talk.

"Hi. My name is Robert and I'm an addict." The man looked down at the podium before continuing. "I've been clean for about three weeks."

"Hi Robert," everyone said in unison.

Sandino immediately burst out laughing, which caused the counselor to give him a very disapproving look.

Narrowing his eyes, the corner of his mouth started to twitch. "Mr. Washington. I do understand that this is your first time with us, but if you can't control yourself I'm going to have to ask you to leave."

Sandino stopped snickering. He hated when anyone tried to play him, especially when they had an audience. "Yeah, my bad."

"Please continue Robert," the counselor stated.

When Robert started talking again, Sandino let out a huge sigh. Irritated, he started to think. *Why the hell did I even come to this fuckin' ridiculous therapy meetin' today in the first place? I don't need this shit.*

Trying to prove to Bryan that he could change and get a team to give him another shot, Sandino had finally agreed to give rehab a try, but the whole experience was already getting on his nerves. Little did he know, the only person crazy enough to deal with him was Skye when they were together even though he resented her for trying to keep him away from his object of desire.

"I started using prescription sleeping pills after a nasty

divorce. At first I started taking them to get some rest just so I could function at work the next day, but then I started taking them to dull the pain of losing my wife," Robert advised.

"Damn, man, you let a woman get to you like that," Sandino interrupted.

"Mr. Washington!" the counselor yelled.

Sandino threw up his hands. "What? I'm just sayin'. I ain't lettin' no bitch drive me that crazy!"

Robert was infuriated. "She wasn't a bitch! She was my wife and I loved her," he shrieked, before lowering his head to eye the wedding ring he still wore.

You could tell by the compassion in his voice that he was still in love with her.

Sandino went on. "Well, where the hell did all that love get you? In here…borin' us to death wit' all of yo' whinin' and shit."

The counselor turned toward Sandino. "So, why are you here?"

"Man…there was a big misunderstandin' and now I have to take this classes to get it all cleared up," Sandino replied.

"Really?" the counselor said with a 'I don't believe that shit look'.

"Yeah! It'll all be cleared up soon though," Sandino said, wiping off his iced out Breitling watch.

The counselor kept digging deeper, but Sandino was too preoccupied with his ringing phone to respond.

"Mr. Washington do you mind? We have a strict no phone policy," the counselor informed.

"I don't care what your policy is. I need to stay contacted wit' my lawyer and my agent at all times," Sandino said, even though he hit the ignore button.

He sat back in his chair looking at everybody like he was bored until his phone rang again. This time he got up and answered it. The counselor was pissed when Sandino walked out of the room with no regard to the other participants.

"Hello," Sandino answered once he entered the hall-way.

"Is this the football star they call Sandino Washington?"

"Who wants to know?"

"Obviously I do."

"Look, who the hell is this? I don't have time to be playin' no games!" he shouted into the phone.

"Oh, it's not a game. You're looking for your family right?"

Sandino paused for a few seconds. "I'm goin' to ask you once again. Who the fuck is this?"

"My name is Mercedes, and I know you're trying to lo-cate your family. You know…Skye, Kareem, Jordan and that pretty baby Payton."

Sandino glanced at the 404 area code and wondered if the bitch on the phone really knew where his family was.

"I'll give you Skye's exact location once you break me off with some money. You can send it Weston Union or fuck-ing Money Gram…however you wanna do it, but I'm not giv-ing you shit for free."

Sandino instantly started yelling. He hated a bitch who asked him for money right off the break. "How the hell did you get my number?"

"I stole it out of my ex's phone. His name is Dre, and that's all the information I'm giving you until I get some money."

Sandino's eyes lit up like a Fourth of July firework dis-play. "Dre? Does he know where Skye is?"

"Hell no, you picked the wrong muthafucka to come find your wife. That weak- ass nigga don't have a clue. Never send a boy to do a man's job. She's right up under his nose, and he doesn't even know it."

"What you mean right under his nose?"

"Skye is fucking his brother, but Dre has no idea"

Sandino almost lost it when she mentioned Skye having sex with another man.

"Are you serious? Who the fuck is the nigga she messin' wit'? I'ma kill 'em!"

"Didn't I tell you that I'm only giving up so much information," Mercedes responded. "Look, we can do a transaction in person if that'll make you feel better. Your wife stole my man. Now, I see why you were beating her ass!"

"Oh really, well I'm comin' to Atlanta, and you better not be fuckin playin' wit' me bitch!" he yelled. "I'm gonna check the flights. My goal is to be there tonight."

"You bring that cash and I'll take you right to that bitch."

They talked a little while longer before Sandino told Mercedes he would pay her once he got to Atlanta. Mercedes even agreed to pick him up from the airport if he needed her to. When Sandino hung up the phone he was beyond heated.

"That nigga Dre didn't do shit. How the fuck is he gonna let a bitch do his job? I'ma get my fuckin' money back as soon as I see his ass."

Trying to get together a plan, he quickly called Cruze, and waited for him to answer.

"Pack a bag nigga, we gotta take a trip. I need you on this one, we gon' bring my family home."

Sandino was aware that Skye didn't like Black so he knew not to include his flunkie on this trip. Besides, she trusted Cruze, which Sandino planned to use in his favor if needed. Sandino ended the call and walked back into the room and took a seat with a big smile on his face.

As he looked around, all he could think about was how much of a loser the people in the meeting were. *Look at all these low life muthafuckas.* Sandino sat and started texting Trina nasty shit on his phone.

His constant moaning and sighing as the counselor lectured them on beating their habits could be heard throughout the room.

"Denial is a massive component of most addictive disorders. It's the denial talking when you laugh the problem off, deny there's a problem, or make excuses for why you abuse drugs," the counselor advised.

Sandino blew out a heavy sigh again. *This muthafucka is really trying my patience.*

The counselor stood up, put his hands in his pockets and paced the floor. "Basically, it's never the addicts fault...it's always someone else's fault," he said, looking right at Sandino.

"Why the fuck did you look at me when you said that shit?" Sandino questioned.

"Mr. Washington, I see you're going to be in rare form every time you come in here!"

"You damn skippy, so get your monkey-ass out my damn face and stop tryna make me talk in these wack-ass meetings."

The counselor certainly didn't expect Sandino's outburst, but it didn't necessarily surprise him. He'd seen it time and time again. Men of Sandino's status not wanting to take responsibility for their actions and admit that they need help came a dime a dozen.

Sandino jumped up from his seat and met the counselor's gaze. "Muthafucka, let me tell yo' ass somethin'. I'm only here because I have to be. I don't have no damn problem, but everybody don't agree with me so I gotta sit through this bullshit for a couple more weeks then I'm out. I don't need to be here. I'm Sandino Washington, and don't you forget it!" he yelled, before leaving the room.

Chapter Twenty~Six

Jumping into his car, Justice pulled away faster than he should've been going down his residential street. Even though he tried to sleep the anger off after Skye kicked him out the night before, he still couldn't stomach what Mercedes had possibly done. He'd seen some foul shit in his day, but all the conniving things Mercedes were involved in lately pressed down hard on his chest. He clinched his teeth all the way to her house as thoughts of Skye's face when she told him to leave replayed in his mind. The thought of him losing her for good all because of Mercedes' unstable-ass, made his blood boil.

Justice's adrenaline had reached its peak by the time he arrived at Mercedes' apartment and power walked to her building. Pounding on the door, Justice wondered how she could do something so malicious. He was fed up with all her childish games and the fact that she was willing to bring harm to Skye just to be with him. Mercedes needed to be put in her place once and for all.

When she didn't answer, Justice started kicking the door with this boot this time. Her nosy neighbor's even thought it was the police and immediately started coming outside, one by one, looking at him like he was crazy. However, Justice could care less.

One girl who came to the door wearing a dirty scarf on her head and some ripped pajamas started yelling when she saw Justice banging.

"You need to get yo' ass out of here before I call the police."

She held her cell phone up so Justice could see she was serious.

"Bitch… shut the hell up and go back in your apartment. This does not concern you."

"Nigga, you don't know me so don't be talkin' to me like that!"

"I don't wanna know you. Now, take your ass back in the house," Justice responded.

A few minutes later Mercedes opened the door completely naked with a smile on her face.

Oh shit, here we go, Justice thought. He was in no mood for her antics.

"To what do I owe this honor? You finally came to your senses huh?" she asked.

Justice pushed his way into her apartment without even answering. Seconds later, he grabbed Mercedes naked body, pushed her on the couch then placed his hands around her neck and pressed hard.

"Why did you do it? You went too fucking far this time!" he tightened his grip letting her know he meant business.

Mercedes tried to fight back, but once she realized she couldn't handle him, she screamed as much as she could.

"Get…off…me Justice!"

"Shut the hell up!" Justice slapped Mercedes across the face catching her off guard. The stinging sensation and ringing in her ear followed the blow.

"I should've sent somebody over here to violate your crazy-ass. That shit you did to Skye was fucked up! What the hell is wrong with you?" he yelled then smacked her again.

At that moment, Dre ran out the bedroom in a pair of checkered boxers completely confused after hearing Mercedes scream along with their scuffle.

"What's going on? Get off her Deuce!" Dre attempted to pull his brother away.

"Stay out of this!" Justice yelled.

When Dre managed to pull them apart, he turned to his brother who was out of breath and foaming at the mouth.

"Deuce, what's wrong wit' you. She's a female, not some nigga on the street."

"I told you this bitch was crazy. She had something to do with my girl getting raped. She actually had a man go over her house and…rape her. She needs help!" Justice ranted.

Mercedes stood up and grabbed her neck. *At least I know that shit worked*, she thought. She quickly formed a smirk on her face before acting like she was distraught again. "You're a fucking liar Justice. Why would I do something like that? You're just mad because I'm not checking for your ass any more."

Justice lunged at her, but Dre held him back.

"You can stay with the bitch for all I care. I'm back with Dre anyway," Mercedes said then displayed a devilish grin.

"Yeah right bitch, that shit is all a front," Justice said jumping back at her.

She quickly ducked behind Dre for protection.

"Look man, I don't know what you talkin' about, and I damn sure don't know anything about your girl bein' raped. I can handle Mercedes from now on. I suggest you go back to your girl. I got 'dis over here," Dre suggested.

Justice couldn't believe what he was hearing. "So, you gone believe that crazy bitch over me? Your own brother!" He finally looked down at Dre's boxers. "I can't believe you over here fucking her anyway after I told the type of shit I've been going through with her. I see you're still dumb and making stupid-ass decisions. I guess some things will never change," Justice said, shaking his head. "Y'all deserve each other!"

Insulted, Dre walked up on his brother like he was a stranger. "Nigga, fuck you! Ever since we were teenagers you been thinkin' you better than me. You do dirt just like I do. Does anybody at the shelter know dat fake-ass college degree on your wall is some bullshit? Dats why your wife almost left your ass when y'all first got married. You stole her money."

"I didn't steal shit. Don't get mad at me because I'm a better business man than you," Justice responded.

Suddenly, the two brothers got into a shoving match that soon turned into an amateur WWE Wrestling event. They locked onto one another as Dre hemmed Justice up against wall causing all the pictures to fall off. Determined not to lose to his baby brother, Justice spun around and pushed Dre into the wooden living room table breaking it into pieces.

Mercedes had a slight grin on her face as she eased away and headed into her bedroom without ever being noticed. In her mind, the fight wasn't about Skye; it was about their love for her. As both brothers rolled over on their backs, they continued arguing about Mercedes as she disappeared.

"No matter how much you try to protect her Dre she needs help. I know she had something to do with Skye getting raped."

Dre laid still on the floor for a minute. "Did you say Skye?"

"Yes, I did. That's my girl's name."

"I thought her name was Janelle."

"No, and it's a long story. She was using a fake name because she was hiding from her husband..."

Dre interrupted Justice "Her husband, Sandino Washington, right?"

Justice turned and looked at his brother. "That's right, I almost forgot you asked me about her that day at the shelter. Why were you asking about my girl, Dre? And don't fucking lie."

Dre finally sat up. "I was hired by Sandino to come and

look for Skye and his kids. I'm supposed to take them back to Miami. I can't believe all 'dis time I've been runnin' around lookin' for her and she was right in front of my face."

"I thought you said you changed?" Justice said in disbelief. "I guess that was just bullshit."

Dre got pissed all over again. "There you go talkin' about some shit you know nothin' about. I have changed. But I couldn't start over broke. Look, I couldn't resist the money he gave me just to come find them. Besides I didn't know she was your girl!"

Justice finally stood up. "Did he want you to kill her?"

Dre shook his head. "No, not at all." He didn't feel the need to tell Justice that Sandino had indeed mentioned that option.

"How much did you get?" Justice questioned. He had to know how much Skye's bounty was worth.

"Twenty thousand. I got half before I left Miami, and I was supposed to get half when I found her."

Justice was speechless. Just as he was about to respond, Mercedes walked back into the living room with a gun in one hand and Dre's belongings in the other.

"Both of y'all muthafuckas get the hell out!" she yelled, pointing the gun toward them.

Dre was beyond shocked. Not only were they having sex again when Justice arrived, but he even believed her when she told Justice they were getting back together. Now she was pointing a loaded .9mm in his face.

"I know you not tryin' to play me after I just kept my brother from whooppin' your ass," Dre said.

"I guess you just took one for the team." When Mercedes tried to give Dre his stuff, he threw up his hands, so she handed everything to Justice. "Trust and believe neither of you have seen the last of me, some shit is about to go down and it's nothing either of you can do about it." She turned to Justice. "I can't believe you came over here and accused me of rape all over that bitch? You'll soon see that she ain't shit!"

Dre didn't even have time to put anything on as she forced both of them to the front door. Mercedes waved the gun. "Both of y'all muthafuckas need to get out...now!"

"You a crazy bitch. I can't believe I fell for your shit once again!" Dre yelled.

"Whatever Dre, I gotta do what I gotta do just like always. If you think I'm gonna allow you to get that money you're wrong!"

❦❦❦❦❦❦❦❦

Skye laid across her bed with so many thoughts floating around in her head. She'd flipped through the channels on the television at least four times, but really couldn't concentrate on anything. She tried desperately to block Justice out of her mind, but wasn't having any luck.

Skye wiped a single tear away from her left eye thinking about how disappointed she was. Skye knew she shouldn't have taken her frustration out on him, but that still didn't hide the fact that if he and Mercedes had never slept together, none of this would've ever happened.

"I'm gonna beat that bitch down when I see her," Skye said out loud. She looked up when she heard a knock at her bedroom door.

"Who is it?"

"It's me, Ma," Jordan replied.

"Come in."

Jordan walked in and handed Skye the mail even though the last thing she wanted to see right now was some bills.

"Ma, are you okay? Do you need anything?" Jordan asked concerned then kissed her on the cheek.

"You're so sweet. I'm okay baby, is Payton sleeping?

"No, she's in there playing with Kareem."

"Kareem...really?" Skye was completely surprised. He

218

hardly ever helped out with the baby.

"Yeah, he just got off the phone talking to that dirty girl from across the hall."

"As long as his ass is in the house and staying out of trouble I don't care who he talks to."

Jordan smirked as he left his mom's room.

Skye tossed the mail onto her nightstand. However, one piece of mail in particular caught her eye. It was in a purple colored envelope with her name on it, but didn't have a return address. Trying to figure out what it was, Skye quickly opened it up. Her heart damn near dropped when she saw a picture of Justice and some woman on what looked like their wedding day with a huge red heart drawn around the picture.

As if that wasn't bad enough, it had a note attached that read,

And you thought you knew your man…guess not. How does it feel knowing Justice belongs to someone else? Well, I feel the same way!
Mercedes

In complete shock, Skye dropped the picture on the floor and grabbed her cell phone. Justice was driving to the shelter in deep thought when his phone rang. As soon as he looked at the caller ID and saw Skye's name, he immediately started smiling. He hoped she was calling to tell him to come back over so they could make up.

Make up sex is the best sex, he thought.

"Hey baby," he said answering the phone. He listened to what sounded like Skye balling in the phone. "What's wrong Skye?"

"I need you to be honest with me. Are you married Justice?"

Justice was shocked and wondered where she got that information from.

"Why are you asking me that?" he asked.

"Just answer the fucking question. Are you married?"

she yelled.

Justice paused. He didn't want to lie to her anymore. "Yes, it's true."

"How could you do this to me? You said you wanted to spend the rest of your life with me. How were you supposed to do that if you're another woman's husband? I trusted you!" Skye began to yell. "I should've never let you get close to me. Stay away from my family. I never want to see you again!" she screamed in the phone and hung up.

Chapter Twenty‑Seven

Mercedes paced back in fourth in the terminal at Harts‑field-Jackson Airport waiting for Sandino's flight to land. After Justice and Dre left her apartment that morning, she'd gotten a call from Sandino telling her he was taking a 7:50 p.m. and would arrive by 10:00 p.m. He also made it ab‑solutely clear that she better be on time because he hated to be kept waiting.

After getting a soda, Mercedes took a seat in one of the hard airport chairs and smiled. She couldn't wait to get her hands on that money Sandino was offering for his wife. At that moment, all type of plans starting jumping around in her head. Once she got her sons out of jail, she also planned to go on a much needed shopping spree, then move into a nicer apart‑ment.

She'd hoped that Justice would've come to his senses by now, but after he put his hands on her he was lucky she hadn't slit his throat. She now had another man on her mind, and it damn sure wasn't Dre either. It was Sandino. Mercedes hoped that she could somehow get him into bed then work her magic on him to get even more of his money.

"I could use another car," she said.

After taking a few sips from her Pepsi, she noticed sev‑eral people coming down the escalator. Some of the travelers had luggage that could hold an elephant, while others had just small carry ons. However Sandino wasn't carrying a single thing. She didn't have any problems spotting him as he stood out amongst all the travelers with his football physique. Eyeing his black sweat suit and LeBron James Nikes, Mercedes stared at him like a fresh piece of meat.

"Damn, he looks even better in person. I would definitely love to fuck his fine-ass. Who is that dude with him though? He didn't mention anything about bringing anyone along," she said to herself.

When they reached the bottom of the escalator, Mercedes who was wearing a tight pair of jeans, a cream sweater and thigh high boots, sashayed right up to the two men.

"Sandino, it's me Mercedes."

He looked her up and down before speaking. He didn't think she would be such a cutie with a nice body, but he brushed it off and kept things professional.

"How was your flight? Did you check a bag? If so, we need to go pick up your bags over there," Skye pointed.

"We don't have any bags, we not plannin' on stayin' that long," Sandino responded.

"Oh okay, I thought you were going stay with me, Poppi," she said, batting her eyes. She still hadn't paid Cruze any attention.

Sandino laughed out loud. "Who the fuck told you that? Let's go I don't have all day, where my wife at?" he asked with a stern look on his face.

"I'll take you to her," Mercedes said. She finally turned and looked at Cruze before she walked off.

Damn, he looks good, too, she thought to herself.

While walking through the airport, Cruze looked around to make sure they weren't being followed. He got a bad vibe from her as soon as Mercedes walked up. Something about her wasn't right.

Both men followed behind her leaving the airport and headed to the parking garage. They watched as she tried to make her ass jiggle with every step. Her thick hips bulged from beneath her denim showcasing her best asset.

When they reached her car, Sandino shook his head thinking, *her name is Mercedes and the bitch is driving an old-ass Ford Explorer.*

When they all got inside, it wasn't long before Mercedes headed toward the highway. After riding for a few minutes Mercedes made sure her chest was positioned just right so Sandino could see her large breasts. She caught him looking a few times and knew if it wasn't for the other guy in the back she might've been able to convince him to stop by her place for a quickie before going to find Skye.

At that moment, Mercedes looked in her rear view mirror. "Hey, you in the back, why do you keep looking at me like that?" she asked Cruze.

"Looking at you like what?" he questioned.

She shrugged her shoulders. "I don't know. Like you don't like me or something."

"Bitch, ain't nobody looking at you, I don't even know you," Cruze replied with an attitude.

"Watch who you calling a bitch. I thought since we're all going to be working together we could at least get along." Mercedes replied.

Sandino was irritated because he could tell already that Mercedes talked too much.

"Look, don't worry about him. Just take us to my wife," Sandino stated.

"Do you have my money?" she snapped.

Sandino shook his head. "Yeah, I got it."

"And I hope you brought enough. I'm not doing this shit for a small amount," Mercedes continued.

"Look, you gettin' on my fuckin' nerves. Don't be tryna tell me how to handle business!" Sandino shot back.

"Okay, it's no need to get nasty. I just wanted to make sure we were clear on the money, that's all. Look under that seat," she said, battering her eyes at him again.

When Sandino reached under the seat, he pulled out her .9mm.

"I thought you might need that," Mercedes said. "If your friend needs one, we can head in another direction."

"Good lookin' out. That was a smart move." Sandino was about to put the gun back under the seat when he felt his phone vibrate. After looking at the number, he quickly decided to take the call. "What up?" Sandino listened for a few seconds before responding. "Okay, bet. That's what's up. I'll hit you back," he said, hanging up the phone. He clapped his hands like he'd just gotten some great news. "So, Mercedes, tell me a little bit more about how you know my wife. How are my kids doin'?"

"Well, it's like I explained to you on the phone, Skye and the kids came to the women's shelter where I used to work. Of course I didn't know who she was at the time. Jordan was doing well before they moved out, but Kareem got locked up for selling drugs."

Mercedes didn't think it was a good idea to mention that Kareem got locked selling drugs for her two sons.

"Kareem got locked up for sellin' drugs? What the fuck was he doin' sellin' drugs? I knew that bitch couldn't handle raisin' my kids on her own." Sandino was beyond furious. "So, you don't work at the shelter anymore?"

"No, I got fired all behind your wife's ass. I told you, she stole my man and he fired me. I caught them in his office having sex one day. Your wife is probably fucking Dre, too," Mercedes lied without a conscious.

She continued to drill Sandino about Skye and Justice knowing it would piss Sandino off. She needed him to be nice and fired up when they got to Skye's.

"Mercedes, I need you to pull over for a second I gotta piss...bad." Sandino said.

"Can't you wait? We don't have long to go," Mercedes

224

advised.

"Unless you want me to piss all over your car, I suggest you stop," Sandino demanded.

After taking the next exit, Mercedes pulled the car over onto the small shoulder. The road was dark and deserted; without a car in sight.

"Be careful it's a lot of ditches around here," she warned.

When Sandino got out the car to take a piss, Mercedes looked in the back at Cruze.

"You alright back there sexy? You're so quiet."

"I'm straight," was all Cruze said back to her.

Once Sandino returned to the car, instead of getting back in the passenger's seat he walked over to the driver's side and told Mercedes to let him drive. "You drivin' too damn slow and I need to get where we were going."

"It's cool, I can continue driving," she responded. "You don't even know where we're going."

"Just get out!" Sandino barked.

Not wanting to fight, Mercedes finally opened the door. *So, he's a gentleman, too*, she thought when Sandino held the driver's door open for her.

"I'm telling you. It would've been easier for me to drive since I know where to…" It was all Mercedes could get out as she hopped into the passenger's side and was met with her own gun staring her in the face.

She looked over at Sandino with terrified eyes. "What…what are you doing?"

With a wicked grin on his face, Sandino said, "What does it look like?"

"But…if you kill me how are going to find your wife and kids?" Mercedes voiced trembled.

"I got the information I need so your services are no longer needed."

Did Dre call and tell him everything, she thought.

Suddenly, the sound of two shots being fired echoed across the silent highway.

"What the fuck!" Cruze yelled. "You trippin' Sandino. Why the hell did you do that? How the fuck are we supposed to find Skye now?" He stared at Mercedes who was now slumped over.

"Didn't you just hear me tell that bitch her services were no longer needed?"

"You out of control. Even if you didn't need her anymore, did you have to kill her?"

"Yes, I did. That bitch talked too much," Sandino replied.

He jumped out the car and ran over to the passenger side then pulled Mercedes' lifeless body out. Looking around, Sandino pushed her over into a nearby embankment before hoping back into the driver's seat.

"Come on nigga. We ain't got all night," he said to Cruze.

Once Cruze hopped up front, Sandino pulled off and raced down the street with screeching tires. He looked over at his friend and passed him the gun.

"Now, it's your turn to go handle that other bitch for me."

Chapter Twenty-Eight 🏈

Dre stepped out the shower in his hotel room and grabbed a huge towel off the rack. Looking around at the elegant marble tile and smoky grey walls, Dre could've stayed in the mini sanctuary the rest of the night. After drying off his body, he walked over to the king size bed and took a seat. In his head, he was still trying to make sense out of the shit that had taken place earlier that day.

Justice jumping on Mercedes and accusing her of getting Skye raped, along with him and his brother actually throwing blows was bad enough. But Mercedes flipping out and pulling a gun on him had put the icing on the cake. He still couldn't believe she'd played him like that. As much as he loved her and seemed to tolerate her crazy ways, some things were just unforgivable. Dre knew it was best he found out now just how crazy she really was instead of later.

As Dre wondered what his next move was, he laid back on the bed still in disbelief how Sandino's wife was actually his brother's girl.

"That shit is too much of a coincidence," he said out loud.

Dre hoped that Justice wasn't too attached to Skye since she really belonged to someone else. *Regardless of how much my brother wants her as his girl, there's no way Sandino is gonna let her go 'dat easy. I might not have found her, but*

Sandino paid me to tell him where she was, so I gotta come through. Ain't no bitch comin' between me and my money.

When Dre stood up to retrieve his cell phone from his pants, suddenly there was a loud knock at the door. Startled, Dre looked out the peephole and to his surprise, the cutie from the front desk that he flirted with when he first checked in was standing at the door with a bottle of cheap champagne and two glasses.

"What up?" Dre asked though the door.

"Since it's your birthday and I saw you get on the elevator alone, I thought you might wanna have a drink with me?" she looked directly into the peephole.

"What the hell I got to lose? Shit, I got a lot of years to make up on gettin' pussy," he said, opening the door.

When she walked in wearing a tight v-neck tunic, Dre was mesmerized by her huge breast.

"Hey, Mr. Jones," she said, calling him by the last name on the fake ID.

"Hey. I would love to have a drink wit' you, but it's not my birthday. Ummm..." Dre realized that he didn't know her name.

"My name is Shana. Oh, my bad...your ID had today's date as your birthday."

Dre had completely forgotten about the fake date. He started shaking his head. "You know what, I feel so stupid. I've been working so hard that I guess I forgot my own damn birthday."

Shana smiled. "It happens."

She walked over to the dresser and placed the glasses down then popped the champagne open. After pouring two drinks, she passed Dre one then they both took a seat on the bed.

"So, what's up," Dre said, taking a sip.

"Well, I'm sure you know that I didn't come here to talk."

Dre displayed a slight grin. "Oh, really. So, what did you come for?"

Putting down her glass, Shana grabbed the bottom of her shirt then pulled it over her head, exposing her bra-less chest. She placed her hands on her hips.

"I came for this."

Dre stared at both of her nipple rings before downing the champagne. "And I'm glad you came."

It didn't take long for them to dive right into a session of hot, passionate sex. Dre didn't know if it was the head she'd given him right before they started fucking doggie style or what, but Shana made him forget all about his problems. She felt so good he'd already claimed her as his new piece of ass.

An hour later, Shana got dressed and told Dre to plug her number into his phone. After searching for his phone and not being able to find it, he finally wrote her number on the hotel pad by the phone. After saying their goodbyes, Shana was about to walk out the door, but suddenly stopped.

"Oh yeah, I forgot to tell you. It was some girl following you the other day. She walked in the lobby after you and watched you get on the elevator. She then asked if I knew what room you were in. When I told her I couldn't give out that information she got mad and left. Let me find out you got a damn stalker." Shana laughed as she walked out the room.

Dre wondered who the hell could've been asking about him. *It had to be Mercedes*, he thought.

He glanced at his clock on the nightstand realizing that he needed to make a run. He didn't have time to take another shower so he washed up and grabbed a pair of white Calvin Klein boxer briefs and quickly got dressed. After looking at himself in the mirror, he grabbed his keys and proceeded to look for his phone once again.

"Where in the hell did I put that shit," he said, patting his coat pockets.

When there was another loud knock on the door, Dre

couldn't help but smile. Figuring it was Shana back for another round, he didn't even bother to look through the peephole. Instead, he swung the door open with a huge smirk. When Dre saw two police officers standing in front of him, the smirk turned into an instant frown.

"Andre Mitchell?" one of the officers asked.

"Ahhh…yes," he responded. "What can I help you wit'?"

"Mr. Mitchell, please place your hands behind your back. You're under arrest!"

They immediately whisked Dre around and handcuffed him.

"For what?" Dre yelled.

"For sexually assaulting Janelle Coleman."

"Are you serious? Dis must be some kind of mistake, I didn't sexually assault anybody!"

"Well, a witness came forward and told us that she saw you going into Ms. Coleman's apartment that day. She picked your picture out of a lineup," the other officer stated. "The witness even demanded that we tell you her name is Mercedes Guzman."

Dre's eyes widened. He'd been locked a few times, so his record wasn't the best, but he could've never been capable of rape. "No, you gotta believe me. I'm innocent, I've been set up!"

"Well, I'm sure you can prove just how innocent you are in court Mr. Mitchell," the taller officer responded.

As the officers began to escort him toward the elevator, Dre dropped his head. He couldn't believe that Mercedes had set him up. If only he could turn back the time, he would've let Justice beat her ass.

Chapter Twenty-Nine

Justice sat in the living room at Skye's apartment pleading with her to forgive him and take him back. He told her he'd planned to tell her about his wife, but the time was never right. Skye had refused to open the door for him at first, but after standing outside banging on her door for almost ten minutes she knew he wouldn't go away and didn't want her neighbors to call the police, so she let him in to hear him out and get the shit over with. She really wasn't in the mood to deal with his lying ass or anybody else for that matter. Jordon and Payton were spending the night with Lydia to give her some time to herself and since Kareem couldn't leave the house, he'd been staying out of her way locked up in his room with his headphones on listening to music.

"Justice, I don't think you seem to understand. I don't want anything else to do with you. You're married!" Skye yelled at him. "You think I wanna deal with this shit right now after getting raped!"

"Baby, look, I don't love her, I love you and I'm so sorry for what happened to you. I even went over and tried to beat Mercedes' ass for what she did to you. Of course she tried to deny the fact that she had anything to do with it, but I didn't believe her. I tried to choke her ass out until my brother came running out her bedroom," Justice explained.

"Your brother? What was he doing over there?"

"I never got a chance to tell you that my brother and Mercedes used to date before he got locked up. I still can't believe he started fucking with her again after I told him how crazy she was."

Skye sat up on the couch with a puzzled look on her face. "Hold up Justice, you mean to tell me you slept with your brothers ex?"

"Yes, that's basically what happened baby, but I don't want to talk about Mercedes anymore. I just wanted to let you know I handled her ass for you. All I want to do is make things right between us. Will you please forgive me?"

Skye laughed and shook her head.

"You're supposed to be helping battered woman and you actually tried to beat one up? Wow this is some Jerry Springer shit I'm dealing with right now. I'm afraid to find out what else you're hiding. Please leave."

Skye layed back down on the couch, grabbed the remote and turned to VH1. She knew they were gonna have some sort of reality TV show to watch.

"Are you sure you want me to go?" Justice asked.

"Yep," Skye replied. She never took her eyes off the TV.

Feeling defeated, Justice got up and walked to the front door. After opening it, he turned around when he realized he'd left his car keys on the table. He looked up when he saw Sandino and Cruze entering Skye's apartment.

"Daddy's home bitch! Didn't I tell you I would hunt you down?" a voice yelled out.

Skye slowly turned her head when she heard the familiar voice, and saw Sandino standing there.

Paralyzed with fear, Skye sat there for what seemed like forever until she finally jumped up and ran behind Justice for protection.

"Look Sandino, don't come to my home with that bullshit, I've moved on with my life now. I have a good man who loves me right here." Skye nervously grabbed Justice by the arm when she noticed the gun in Cruze's hand.

"Oh really? Is this what you call a fuckin' home?" Sandino looked around her small apartment with disgust. "This is a dump. I can't believe you put my kids through this bull-shit. And let me give you a word of advice since I see you're still a dumb bitch and yo' monkey-ass can't do shit right. You need to be careful who you let into your bed! Ain't that right Justice?"

Justice lowered his head and walked over beside Sandino.

"You see baby, your lil' boyfriend sold you out. Money can buy anything or should I say anybody!" Sandino said with a loud, vicious laugh.

Skye looked at Justice with tears in her eyes. "How could you?"

"I already told you…money sweetheart." Sandino looked at Justice. "Tell her how you did it."

"No, I don't think that's…"

Cruze pointed the gun at Justice, cutting him off. "Tell her! Don't bitch out now!" he yelled.

Justice lowered his head again. "I managed to get Dre's phone when we were at Mercedes' house this morning, so I called your husband. I told him that I knew where you were."

"And what else?" Sandino said with authority.

"I gave him your address and told him that I would come into the apartment first, get you comfortable then leave the door open."

By this time, the tears were falling at a rapid pace. "Why?" Skye yelled.

"I needed the money," Justice admitted in a low tone. "I'm about to lose the shelter and my wife if I don't get this gambling habit under control."

"I know this is the nigga who you been fuckin', but I'ma look past all that shit since he…"

At that moment, Skye took off running toward her bedroom, but Sandino quickly caught up with her. Just like old times, he immediately slapped her across the face and grabbed her hair.

"I told you bitch, till death do us part," he whispered in her ear.

As Skye began to scream, Kareem suddenly burst into the room pointing Skye's gun directly at his father.

"Get your hands off my mother before I shoot your ass!" Kareem yelled.

Sandino looked at his oldest son; it was like looking in the mirror. He'd grown taller and picked up some weight and even had a bit of facial hair now.

"Hey, Kareem. Damn son, you've gotten big." Sandino released the grip he had on Skye's hair and walked toward him.

"Didn't I tell you not to move? Stay back!" Kareem shouted.

"Oh, so you think you're a fuckin' man now, you wanna challenge me? I heard about you gettin' locked up. I guess that finally gave you some balls huh, lil'nigga?" Sandino responded.

"You need to leave!" Kareem yelled.

"Sandino…please just leave us alone," Skye begged.

Both Cruze and Justice watched the drama unfold like a Lifetime movie.

As Sandino gazed at Kareem's eyes, he could still see the fear in them. He knew his son wasn't ready to go up against him, so Sandino jumped and tried to grab the gun from Kareem, causing it to go off.

A few seconds later Justice fell to the floor.

Skye screamed, and ran over to Justice's body only to find a bullet hole right in his chest. When she looked back toward her son, she saw him and Sandino scuffling on the floor for the gun.

All of a sudden a gun shot went off. Terrified that Kareem might be hurt, Skye immediately made her way over to her son and checked his body.

"Kareem…Kareem, are you okay? Oh my God!" she screamed.

"I'm okay, Ma." he said out of breath.

Seconds later, Skye looked over and saw Sandino bleeding from the back of his head. She also noticed that her gun had slid to the other side of the room. Puzzled, Skye looked up wondering how Sandino could've been shot. That is until she looked over at Cruze who had a gun pointed in Sandino's direction.

"I told you, I got you. Sandino had to be stopped!" Cruze finally said.

Coming Soon

NEXT DOOR Nympho

A NOVEL BY C.J. HUDSON

In Stores May 2011
The Final Chapter...

PO Box 423
Brandywine, MD 20613
301-362-6508

FAX TO:
301-579-9913

ORDER FORM

Ship to:	
Address:	
City & State:	Zip:

Date: _____ Phone: _____
Email: _____

Make all money orders and cashiers checks payable to: **Life Changing Books**

Qty.	ISBN	Title	Release Date	Price
	0-9741394-2-4	Bruised by Azarel	Jul-05	$ 15.00
	0-9741394-7-5	Bruised 2: The Ultimate Revenge by Azarel	Oct-06	$ 15.00
	0-9741394-3-2	Secrets of a Housewife by J. Tremble	Feb-06	$ 15.00
	0-9741394-6-7	The Millionaire Mistress by Tiphani	Nov-06	$ 15.00
	1-934230-99-5	More Secrets More Lies by J. Tremble	Feb-07	$ 15.00
	1-934230-98-7	Young Assassin by Mike G.	Mar-07	$ 15.00
	1-934230-95-2	A Private Affair by Mike Warren	May-07	$ 15.00
	1-934230-94-4	All That Glitters by Ericka M. Williams	Jul-07	$ 15.00
	1-934230-93-6	Deep by Danette Majette	Jul-07	$ 15.00
	1-934230-96-0	Flexin & Sexin Volume 1	Jun-07	$ 15.00
	1-934230-92-8	Talk of the Town by Tonya Ridley	Jul-07	$ 15.00
	1-934230-89-8	Still a Mistress by Tiphani	Nov-07	$ 15.00
	1-934230-91-X	Daddy's House by Azarel	Nov-07	$ 15.00
	1-934230-88-X	Naughty Little Angel by J. Tremble	Feb-08	$ 15.00
	1-934230847	In Those Jeans by Chantel Jolie	Jun-08	$ 15.00
	1-934230855	Marked by Capone	Jul-08	$ 15.00
	1-934230820	Rich Girls by Kendall Banks	Oct-08	$ 15.00
	1-934230839	Expensive Taste by Tiphani (SOLD OUT)	Nov-08	$ 15.00
	1-934230782	Brooklyn Brothel by C. Stecko	Jan-09	$ 15.00
	1-934230669	Good Girl Gone bad by Danette Majette	Mar-09	$ 15.00
	1-934230804	From Hood to Hollywood by Sasha Raye	Mar-09	$ 15.00
	1-934230707	Sweet Swagger by Mike Warren	Jun-09	$ 15.00
	1-934230677	Carbon Copy by Azarel	Jul-09	$ 15.00
	1-934230723	Millionaire Mistress 3 by Tiphani	Nov-09	$ 15.00
	1-934230715	A Woman Scorned by Ericka Williams	Nov-09	$ 15.00
	1-934230685	My Man Her Son by J. Tremble	Feb-10	$ 15.00
	1-924230731	Love Heist by Jackie D.	Mar-10	$ 15.00
	1-934230812	Flexin & Sexin Volume 2	Apr-10	$ 15.00
	1-934230748	The Dirty Divorce by Miss KP	May-10	$ 15.00
	1-934230758	Chedda Boyz by CJ Hudson	Jul-10	$ 15.00
	1-934230766	Snitch by VegasClarke	Oct-10	$ 15.00
	1-934230693	Money Maker by Tonya Ridley	Oct-10	$ 15.00
	1-934230774	The Dirty Divorce Part 2 by Miss KP	Nov-10	$ 15.00
	1-934230170	The Available Wife by Carla Pennington	Jan-11	$ 15.00
	1-934230774	One Night Stand by Kendall Banks	Feb-11	$ 15.00
	1-934230278	Bitter by Danette Majette	Feb-11	$ 15.00
			Total for Books	$

* Prison Orders- Please allow up to three (3) weeks for delivery.

Shipping Charges (add $4.95 for 1-4 books*) $ _____

Total Enclosed (add lines) $ _____

Please Note: We are not held responsible for returned prison orders. Make sure the facility will receive books before ordering.

*Shipping and Handling of 5-10 books is $6.95, please contact us if your order is more than 10 books. (301)362-6508